To the best wife in the world

on our fifth wedding anniversary.

June 26, 2015

You are my sunshine.

Chapter One

Poor bastard.

Sara Larson's new neighbor had no idea he was going to be castrated today. Nobody messed with her sleep.

Nobody.

She propped herself up on her elbows in bed and listened to the noise that woke her up, a squealing coming through the wall. It was so *not* what she wanted to hear at seven-thirty on a Sunday morning—on the first day of her two-month-long summer vacation. Okay, technically it was the *second* day of her vacation. But how could yesterday really count as a vacation day when she'd spent fifteen hours moving into her new place? Exactly. Didn't count.

She gazed around the bedroom of her new place. Her *amazing* new place. A two bedroom, two bath townhome that was walking distance to downtown Campbell, a quaint Silicon Valley city.

Upside: Beautiful place in a desirable area. Downside: Sharing a common wall with someone who didn't believe—as she did—that weekends were meant for sleeping in.

At least the noise stopped.

Sara rolled onto her side to glance down at the doggie

bed. She stretched her arm out to stroke the head of one of the largest dogs in the world.

"Did the noise wake you too, Kili?"

The two-hundred pound Saint Bernard lifted her head and gratefully accepted her mother's love. Then she exhaled stinky doggy breath into Sara's face and plopped her head back down. Two things were obvious. One, Kili needed a breath mint. And two, the dog wanted to sleep longer.

Me too.

Sara laid her head back down on the pillow, closed her eyes, and tried to drift back to sleep. A few seconds later the annoying racket returned, reverberating through the walls. Louder than before. Sara was sure she could feel the bed vibrating. This was ridiculous.

It's Sunday morning!

Forget about the castration. Someone—with no common sense—was going to die.

Sara smacked the wall swiftly one time with her knuckles. Hopefully that would get them to stop doing whatever they were doing.

The noise continued.

She let out a deep breath and knocked louder—okay, some people would call it banging.

The ruckus stopped.

Yes!

A few seconds later she received an unexpected answer from her new neighbor.

Bang! Bang! Bang!

Sara stared at the wall and furled her eyebrows. She wasn't in the mood for this. She couldn't believe the neighbor banged her back. She got on her knees on the bed and returned the bang harder.

Take that!

If the person on the other side of the wall thought this was funny, Sara wasn't laughing. Hands on her hips, she waited for a response.

You better not bang me back again. I swear, if you do…

She received the neighbor's second answer loud and clear.

Bang! Bang! Bang!

Sara huffed and jumped out of bed. This was *not* how she wanted to start off things in her new place.

"Come on, Kili. We're going next door."

The dog didn't budge.

"Cookie!" said Sara.

"Woof!" Kili jumped up and slammed into the nightstand. "Woof!"

Sara leaned over and grabbed hold of the wobbling turquoise ceramic lamp before it toppled over the edge. She let go of the lamp and rubbed the top of Kili's head. "Mommy knows you so well. Come on, I need you to kill someone for me."

Sara was kidding, of course. Kili was a gentle giant and the only thing she might do was lick the person to death.

Still, the dog's size was intimidating to some people. Hopefully she could scare the neighbor a little.

Or a lot.

Sara slid on her jeans and her favorite "Happy" tank top. *Screw the bra, I'm in no mood to care about looks.*

She stepped into her sandals and headed out the door with Kili. "This is the last thing I want to be doing on a Sunday morning. I should be sleeping. Sleeping is healthy. Eight hours a day, that's all. Is that too much to ask for?" Sara realized she was talking in a pretty high volume and didn't want anyone to think she was crazy, so she stopped.

A few steps out the door Kili yanked Sara back to sniff the birch tree out front. She pulled Sara around the tree twice before finding the preferred spot for her morning pee at the base of the tree.

"Good girl."

After Kili finished her business Sara knocked on the front door of the townhome next door and waited. She was ready to give them a piece of her mind. Better to lay down the law now and let the neighbor know where she stood instead of letting things get out of hand.

She leaned in and placed an ear close to the door. She didn't hear any sound or movement inside. No squealing either. But there was an odd noise coming from the outside, close by.

Sara glanced down and watched as Kili chewed on the neighbor's plant. Before she could do anything the entire plant disappeared inside of Kili's mouth. Not even roots were left. Just dirt. Kili stood there grazing like a cow.

Great. Should have fed her before I left home.

She lifted her hand to knock again and was startled by the sound of someone unlocking the door. She dropped her arm and waited. The door slid open, revealing a shirtless man with sky-blue eyes.

Oh dear God in heaven, would you look at that.

The man was positively scrumptious; tall and lean with dark blond medium-length hair that was sticking up in fifty directions of sexy. Sara wasn't sure if he was trying to look sexy on purpose or if it happened naturally. Didn't really matter—her eyes were happy.

"Can I help you?" said the man.

"Uh..."

Odd. Sara had lost the ability to form sentences.

The man tilted his head to the side, obviously waiting for her to stop being a freak. Finally the blood returned to her brain.

He woke you up, remember? Get mad! Stop the chest-gawking and say something!

"I'm your new neighbor next door," she said. "I moved in yesterday."

"Congratulations."

Kili wagged her tail at the sight of the man and tried to pull toward him but Sara kept her steady.

Traitor.

Sara's gaze dropped to the man's arms that were covered with mud. What a slob. Who walked around their home with mud on their arms? Not that it mattered to her. She was there to give him a piece of her mind. He woke her up at seven-thirty on a Sunday morning and there was hell to pay.

Take your eyes off his broad shoulders and toned biceps and let him have it!

The man's gaze dropped to Kili. "Cute pony. You ride it over?"

Sara's lips quivered. She wasn't going to give this sexy, muddy, noise-making neighbor's ego the satisfaction of her laughter. She needed to focus.

"What the…" The man's eyes traveled to the planter box on his porch where he used to have a beautiful, healthy, alive plant. His eyes shifted to Kili, who was still chewing. "Does your pony need a toothpick?"

Crap.

Kili had a satisfied look on her face and was now licking her chops. "Her name is Kili and I think it's obvious she's a dog. And yes, she ate your plant. I'm sorry. I'll get you a new one."

The man shook his head. "That's not necessary. But you may want to tell her this isn't a salad bar."

Sara felt all of a sudden she had less power after what Kili had done but she was going to stay the course and tell the neighbor off. Time to get down to business.

"You woke me up this morning with a strange noise

coming from your place," she said.

"I woke you up?"

"Yes. So, whatever you're doing in there…" She eyed the mud on his arms. "…wrestling alligators or whatever—could you please keep it down or at least wait until a decent hour before you start disrupting my peace?"

The man analyzed Sara for a moment and chuckled. "Disrupting your peace?"

"Yes."

He nodded and seemed to be considering his inconsiderate actions. Good. Hopefully he felt terrible and was going to apologize now.

"What about you disrupting *my* peace?" he asked.

"What are you talking about?"

"Your pony—"

"Quit calling her that."

"*Kili* was barking last night." At the sound of her name, Kili pulled hard and licked the man's legs. He smiled and patted her on the head. "Hi, girl."

Sara wasn't going to cut the guy any slack because he liked dogs. Lots of people liked dogs. And many were much better looking than this man. Okay, maybe that part wasn't true. This guy was super-model-take-my-breath-away-cover-of-*People*-magazine gorgeous. But his good looks weren't going to get him anywhere. No way. Besides, the man was lying about Kili barking last night. Time to set the record straight and put him in his place.

"She wasn't barking last night," said Sara. "It had to be some other dog."

"It was definitely your dog," he said, continuing to stroke Kili. "But did I come over and say anything to you? No. Why? Because I'm a nice person."

"Impossible."

"You're saying I'm not nice?"

"What? No! I mean, I have no idea! I don't even know you, so don't try to twist my words around. I'm saying it's *impossible* that Kili was barking last night. She was with me the *entire* night and she didn't bark. Not once."

"You're mistaken."

"No. I'm not."

"She wasn't with you when you went to pick up Chinese food."

"She—"

Sara thought for a moment.

Crap.

He was right. Sara had left Kili alone on the back patio while she went to go pick up the egg rolls and chow mein.

Wait a minute. How did he know I went to get Chinese food?

"Were you spying on me?" she asked.

The man laughed. "Dream on…"

"You think this is funny?"

He pointed to her Happy shirt. "Were they all out of Grumpy?"

Sara stared him down. "My dog can swallow you

whole."

"Right." He pointed to his empty planter box. "She's a vegetarian, obviously. Is there anything else I can help you with this morning? I have work to do."

She stared at him for a few seconds and blinked. "No."

"Good," he said.

"Fine."

"Perfect."

"Better than perfect."

"Good."

He smirked. "You already said that."

*****

Ian McBride closed the front door before his new neighbor could say another word. He peeked out the window and watched her go back to her place. If she wasn't so crabby she'd definitely be his type. Petite, around five-seven, blonde hair, toned body, and lots of energy.

Too bad the energy was negative.

Still, she was a beautiful woman and he had great difficulty maintaining eye contact with her since it was obvious she wasn't wearing a bra. Forget about being beautiful—she was hotter than hell. He saw her move in yesterday and assumed she was a pleasant person since she whistled as she carried boxes in from the moving truck.

Bad assumption.

He needed to cut her some slack since he knew how exhausting moving was. She had a right to complain about the noise too—he felt bad about waking her up. What about all of the noise her dog made last night? Okay, maybe he exaggerated that part a little but he had to think of *something* when she started copping an attitude. The truth was, he was frustrated with his current project and shouldn't have taken it out on her.

He returned to his spare bedroom and sat on the stool in front of the potter's wheel. He knew the neighbor was complaining about the noise the machine made. What do you expect from something manufactured in the fifties? He had to admit the odd noises were a bit annoying at times but he couldn't see himself getting rid of the machine—it was too sentimental to him. His Uncle Stephen was a famous sculptor who had left the potter's wheel to Ian after he'd passed away. He'd taught Ian everything he knew. Ever since he could remember Ian had wanted to be like his uncle. The way he molded clay was a gift. Sure, there were many talented sculptors in the world but Stephen was something special; his fingers were magical. And he always believed in Ian, unlike his father. Thoughts of his father's harsh words returned.

You're not good enough. If I couldn't do it, what makes you think you can do it?

He shook off the thoughts and sat down to start work again on the lighthouse sculpture, a gift he would present to his grandparents on their fiftieth anniversary. The last two lighthouses he'd made never made it past the drying stage—they started warping almost immediately. It had to do with the pieces drying too fast and the temperature of the room, so he trashed them both.

Hopefully the third time would be the charm.

Ian analyzed the picture he took of the lighthouse in San Simeon and got to work. He grabbed a chunk of clay, threw some water on top, and started up the wheel again. A few seconds later he heard a knock on the wall, followed by Kili's bark. He continued molding the clay to shape the bottom part of the tower. He wondered who was cuter, the dog or the dog's owner.

Tough call.

He continued to mold the clay and thought of his planter box out front. The truth is, he really didn't mind that Kili ate his plant. He wasn't going to tell his new neighbor that. Not having the plant meant it wouldn't die on him like the last one.

He stopped the potter's wheel and let out a deep breath.

You're not good enough.

He grabbed the clay and hurled it against the wall. It made a loud thump and stuck there for a few moments. Then it plopped to the floor. Total crap.

Bang! Bang! Bang!

Ian stood up and yelled at his new neighbor through the wall, "You can't three-bang me. I invented the three-bang!"

He wasn't in the mood for her nonsense and was frustrated—he needed to finish the lighthouse. Did that woman have a stick up her ass?

He got his answer a few seconds later.

Bang! Bang! Bang!

Yup. A giant stick.

He rinsed his hands, wiped them on a towel, and headed to the kitchen. Grabbing a pot from the bottom cupboard and a wooden spoon from the drawer, he headed back to the other room. He stared at the wall for a brief moment, contemplating what he was about to do. There was a good possibility it wouldn't be considered rational or mature.

Tough shit, she started it.

He raised the wooden spoon above his head and with all his force brought it back down hard against the bottom of the pot several times. He stopped when he realized he could inflict permanent damage on his ear drums.

Ian jumped when he heard the sound of the doorbell.

He let out a deep breath. "Round two." He marched to the front door and swung it open. Unfortunately the door slipped out of his hand and slammed into the wall. He pulled hard a few times to dislodge the door handle from the wall and eyed the baseball-sized hole—drywall and bits of paint falling to the floor.

His new neighbor had returned, this time without the pony. She had her hand over her mouth, looking like she was trying to hold back laughter.

"This isn't funny," he said, pointing to the hole in his wall. "That's your fault."

"How so?"

"It never would have happened if you hadn't come over here."

"Right. I take full responsibility for what my dog did to your plant but this issue you have with your door was brought on by your lack of self-control. You might want to see a doctor about that."

Did she just eye my zipper?

"You think that's funny?" he asked.

"As a matter of fact I do."

"Right. Hilarious."

Ian's cell phone rang and he pulled it from his front pocket.

Billy. His best friend.

"Hey, what's up?" said Ian into the phone, not breaking eye contact with his crabby neighbor.

"Good morning, sunshine," said Billy. "How's my favorite guinea pig?"

Billy was a science teacher and worked at the same school where Ian taught art. He was always experimenting with something, trying to invent the next big thing. Unfortunately he liked to test everything on Ian. Yesterday Billy sprayed Ian with his latest invention, a cologne that also had the recommended daily allowance of vitamins and minerals. It wasn't until after he sprayed Ian that he told him it also had pheromones to attract the opposite sex.

"Are you there?" asked Billy.

"Yeah—I'm quarreling with the new neighbor," said Ian. "She moved in yesterday and already thinks she owns the entire neighborhood."

She stood there, tapping one of her feet on the ground.

"She's not responding to the cologne then?" asked Billy.

Ian studied his neighbor again. She was now grinding her teeth. "Not even close."

"Okay, okay," asked Billy. "Keep monitoring activity from everyone all around you. She's just one person and it can vary from person to person. Back to the woman—is she hot?"

Very.

"Is she hot?" Ian purposely repeated the question back to Billy out loud, hoping to irritate his neighbor. Then he decided to take it a step further by checking her out from head to toe. He crinkled his nose like he smelled something rancid. "She's okay. Her dog's much cuter and less temperamental."

She took a step forward and looked like she was going to hit Ian. He jumped back and slammed into the door, causing the handle to lodge back into the wall again. He yanked it back out and stared at her.

She smiled. "Wimp."

"Hold on, Billy. My neighbor has resorted to name-calling now." Ian lowered the phone down to his side and stared down the woman. "What are you going to do next? Pull my hair?"

She chuckled and then threw a hand over her mouth.

"Billy, Billy. You should see this—she's got teeth!" And damn, she was beautiful when she showed them off. "Hang on." Ian dropped the phone away from his mouth again to address his neighbor. "Excuse me, Mrs. McCoy. Can we continue this feud a little later on? Great, thanks then. Buh-bye."

He closed the door on her before she could speak another word.

"Okay, Billy. What's up? You wanted to talk about the cologne?" Ian peeked out the window and watched the woman walk away.

"No. I actually have something new I've been working on. I want to hook up electrodes to your head. Then I'll inject small, evenly-distributed electromagnetic charges into that thick block of yours."

Ian pictured himself strapped to a chair. "You want to electrocute me?"

"No. Sort of. Yes. But it's not as bad as you think."

"Are you going to rattle off the positives of being electrocuted? Sorry—not gonna happen."

"I think I've found a way to stimulate hair growth."

There was no way Ian was going to be a part of this experiment. That's what rats were for.

"Think of all the bald men," Billy continued. "You'd be

helping them!"

"No," said Ian. "My follicles are still producing fantastically, thank you very much. You need a bald man for this." He couldn't believe he was having this conversation. He needed to get back to working on the lighthouse.

"Where's your sense of adventure?" asked Billy. "I tried it on my bikini area and it worked great! Now I need to try more difficult areas."

"Okay, first, *guys* don't have bikini areas. And number two, you *want* to have more hair…down there?"

"You're missing the point and you're no fun."

"If being electrocuted means I'm fun, I don't want to be fun."

"Fine. Meet me at Katie Bloom's then for a drink."

Katie Bloom's was a cool local Irish-themed pub down the street. The last time the two met there Billy got Ian drunk and somehow convinced him that he should try a new self-tanning pill he was trying to perfect. Ian looked like a pumpkin had thrown up all over him.

"Nice try," said Ian. "I'm not falling for that again."

Billy sighed. "Okay, okay. Then meet me at Mama Mia's. We need to celebrate being off for the summer with a great meal. Better?"

Billy and Ian both were teachers, so he had no problem celebrating the summer. Especially at one of his favorite Italian restaurants.

"*That* I can do. What time?"

KISSING FROGS

"Seven. I'll bring the electrodes."
"Not funny."

Chapter Two

Sara returned home and decided not to get back into bed. She was wide-awake now. The best thing to do would be to have some breakfast and get an early start on unpacking the last few boxes. The noise that woke her up was bad enough, but that loud banging a few minutes ago almost sent her over the edge. It was like the guy was trying to piss her off on purpose.

She sat at the kitchen table with her coffee and toasted bagel with cream cheese. She eyed the Whole Foods canvas shopping bag on the counter, filled with over six weeks of mail. She'd been so busy preparing for the move that she kept all of her mail in that bag without opening it. Luckily she paid all of her bills automatically online, so she didn't have to worry about that. But it was time to sort through the other things and make sure she had given everyone her new address. She tossed a few things in the recycling bin and froze, staring at the next envelope in the stack. A wedding invitation. There's no mistaking those envelopes.

Who the heck is getting married?

Sara only knew two people who were single. Tiffany and Becky. The last time she talked to Tiffany was over six months ago and she wasn't dating anyone at the time. And most men didn't get her friend Becky, so she knew it wasn't her. She opened up the envelope and slid out the contents. She set the silky paper aside and read the card.

No!

Tiffany was getting married.

Sara was happy for Tiffany, but the thought of attending another wedding was going to make her physically ill. She would much rather have all of her teeth removed with pliers. The last two weddings she attended were disasters. At the first wedding Sara was the only single person there, so the bride didn't even toss out the bouquet. She just shrugged, handed the bouquet to Sara, and said, "Your time will come." The next wedding was worse. Sara had to sit at the kids table. She even had her own crayons and a coloring book.

Sara knew she had to attend Tiffany's wedding. The two of them have had an unhealthy competition since freshman year in high school. If Sara accomplished something Tiffany would find a way to top it. Sara was embarrassed to admit that she did the exact same thing when Tiffany shared an accomplishment. She can't remember how the competition started but they had been rivals for almost twenty years. Not a surprise at all Tiffany had sent that invitation. It was almost as if Tiffany was saying, "Top that!"

Maybe Sara *would* top that. But how? Only one way. Bring a man to the wedding so gorgeous that the only thing

Tiffany could do was slap herself.

Wait, how old are we again?

Yeah. Pathetic. But it wasn't going to stop Sara from bringing some hunk to the wedding.

Sara had opened up an online dating account a few months ago and chatted with a few guys who showed some promise. She had over forty guys ask her out and went out with a couple of losers last month. She decided to put a hold on the dating until after the move. This was the perfect excuse to start accepting some of those date requests again. She was going to find the perfect date for Tiffany's wedding—no way in hell she was going by herself again. Not this time.

She popped open her laptop and signed into the dating website. Calvin seemed like a great guy and had asked her out twice, so she was going to accept.

A couple of swapped messages and they were set. Sara and Calvin were going to meet this evening for an Italian dinner. It was a little last-minute, but she was okay with that. She was on a mission to find someone to take to Tiffany's wedding. Had she opened the invitation when it had arrived she would've had more time to browse for the perfect guy. Now, because of her procrastination, she had less than a month until the wedding.

*****

KISSING FROGS

Later in the evening Sara entered Mama Mia's and was immediately waved over by Calvin, who was already seated. His online profile said he had black hair but she had no way to confirm that since he wore a baseball cap in every single picture. He never mentioned sports, so she wondered if he was bald underneath that cap. She wasn't hell-bent against sports—she'd attended a few Sharks and Giants games in the past and had a good time. But she didn't want to date a guy who was obsessed with sports—a guy who would pass up a romantic day trip to Carmel because there was an "important" football game on. *All* of the games were important. Hopefully Calvin wasn't one of those guys.

Tonight would be the right time to ask since he was wearing a Giants cap in the restaurant. That seemed in poor taste, considering this was a first date. She tried not to judge him because he was sweet in their email exchanges—always talking about his mother.

What the heck?

She approached the table and spotted an older woman sitting next to Calvin.

Please don't tell me he brought his mother. Please, no, no, no, no.

Calvin stood up, held out his hand, and smiled. "Hi Sara, a pleasure to meet you."

Sara accepted his limp handshake. "Nice meeting you too." She couldn't help let her eyes drift over to the woman who was still seated. Obviously Calvin noticed.

"Oh!" he said. "Where are my manners?" He pointed to

the woman. "Sara, this is my mother, Gertrude. I hope you don't mind I brought her with me."

"Why would she mind?" asked Gertrude. "Unless she's got something to hide…"

Sara's mind started drifting.

Wasn't Hamlet's mother named Gertrude? Hamlet was obsessed with his mother too.

Hmmm.

The feeling in her gut was telling Sara that this was going to be her first and last date with Calvin. The man really brought his mother on their date. Her first impression of Calvin was he was a mama's boy. Her second impression was that she needed to get through this date as fast as possible. She knew she and Calvin were going nowhere. She still wanted to see what he had underneath that hat. She summoned the energy from somewhere in her body and forced a smile.

"How sweet you came along," Sara lied to Gertrude.

Gertrude eyed Sara from head to toe. "My son is worth a hundred million dollars, Tara."

"It's Sara."

"If you prefer Sara, that's fine. As for my son, I need to approve everything he does, including who he goes out with."

Sara chuckled. This was obviously a joke.

"Did I say something funny?" asked Gertrude.

Calvin cleared his throat and pulled out the chair for

Sara. "Please have a seat. Let's not be so formal here."

Sara sat and picked up the menu. She was big fan of Italian food. A big plate of pasta and a glass of wine would really hit the spot.

"Oh," said Calvin, pulling the menu from Sara's hand. "I took the liberty of ordering your dinner for you."

Oh God. "Really?" asked Sara. "Uh…what am I having?"

Calvin picked up the bottle of Chianti from the table and poured her a glass. "I was going to surprise you, but—"

"You don't have to tell her, son," said Gertrude. "Spontaneity is the spice of life."

Sara wasn't going to tell Gertrude that her son pre-planned the evening's spontaneity. She crossed her fingers that the food coming would be something she liked. Let's face it, she loved just about everything Italian. It was one of her favorite cuisines.

"I hear you're a teacher," said Gertrude.

Sara took a sip of her Chianti. "Yes, Geography. Although we started our summer vacation yesterday."

"You must be looking forward to the time off," said Calvin, adjusting his baseball cap and grimacing.

"I am. Very much so."

"You don't get paid anything during the summer," said Gertrude.

"Uh…" Sara scratched the side of her face. "I'm sorry, was that a question or a statement?" She took a sip of her Chianti and waited for Gertrude to respond.

"A question and I'm sure of the answer. You're looking for a sugar-daddy."

Sara choked and Calvin slapped her on the back. She grabbed her cloth napkin and wiped her mouth.

"Mother," said Calvin. "I've chatted with Sara a few times online. She's not the gold digger-looking-for-a-sugar-daddy type. Are you okay, Sara?"

Sara nodded and nervously wiped her mouth even though she knew it was already dry. "I'm fine."

"Good."

The waiter arrived with the food. He placed the first one plate down in front of Gertrude. "Eggplant Parmesan for the lady." The second plate went to Calvin. "Pasta marinara for the gentleman." He winked at Sara. "Your dish is on the way." The waiter turned and grabbed the last sizzling platter from another waiter and placed it in front of Sara. "Here we go. Festa Dei Sette Pesci."

Sara stared at the plate. "Fish?"

The waiter smiled proudly. "Not just any fish! This is the feast of seven fishes! Enjoy!

Sara stared at the plate.

"Looks great!" said Calvin.

"I'm sorry," said Sara, pushing the plate away before she broke out in hives "I really appreciate you going through the trouble of all of this, but I'm allergic to fish."

Gertrude stared at Sara. "How could you be allergic to fish?"

Sara stared at Gertrude for a moment. "How? Well, I'm really not exactly sure *how* allergies work."

Gertrude glared at Sara as if she had a third eye. "Fish is a staple in our family. We came from a humble family of fisherman, generations ago, and we celebrate fish every day. Our family has built from the ground up one of the largest fish wholesalers in the United States. We pray to the fish gods every night before bed."

Sara wasn't going to take this from her. "How come you're not eating fish this evening then?"

Gertrude opened her mouth and closed it.

Gotcha!

"Okay, Mom," said Calvin. "We don't need to make her feel bad. This is rather unfortunate, though."

Gertrude pointed to Sara's fish feast. "I have an idea. Give me your plate."

Sara looked to Calvin, then back to Gertrude. "Okay."

The woman wasn't so bad after all if she was going to swap plates with her. Sara handed Gertrude her plate and left her hand extended over the table.

"What?" asked Gertrude.

Sara blinked. "Oh. I thought we were going to trade plates."

The Eggplant Parmesan looked delicious.

"What?" Gertrude looked down at her plate. She carved a bite of the food with her fork and stuck it in her mouth. "No, no." She chewed and then moaned. "This is *so* good!

Just order something else, Tara."

"It's Sara."

"As you wish."

Sara sighed and grabbed a piece of bread and dipped it in the olive oil. After a couple of chews she waved the waiter over.

The waiter came rushing over and stared at the plates on the table. "What happened? Is there a problem?"

"No," said Sara. "I'm allergic to fish." She pointed to Gertrude. "She's going to eat my dinner."

"Not a problem at all. I will take *her* plate and—"

The waiter reached to grab the Eggplant Parmesan and Gertrude slapped his hand. "Get away."

The waiter mouthed the word "ouch" and rubbed his hand. He then turned to Sara. "Okay then. I'll have the kitchen make something for you quickly. What would you like?"

Sara stared at Gertrude's plate. "Eggplant Parmesan."

The waiter glanced at Gertrude's plate and then nodded. "As you wish."

Sara smiled and took a sip of her Chianti. The waiter was kind. She could tell by his body language that he didn't approve of Gertrude either.

Technically Calvin hadn't been rude to Sara so she didn't want to be rude to him by getting up and leaving. Yeah, that wasn't a cool move to bring his mother, but he seemed kind. All she had to do was make conversation with these two until the dinner came. Then she would eat and be out of there in no time flat. The things she had to go through to find a date for the wedding.

Sara stared at Calvin's baseball cap.

What are you hiding under there?

She'd guessed it was a head of gray hair or a shiny dome of baldness. If she was going to put money on it, she'd say the bald head.

Sara forced a smile and pointed at the baseball cap. "You're a big Giants fan I see."

Calvin adjusted his cap and winced. "Ouch. Not really. I just…like wearing hats."

The guy is in pain. Must be a recent addition of hair plugs.

Gertrude cleared her throat. "What kind of retirement plan do teachers have these days?"

Okay, where did that question come from?

It was almost as if Gertrude was trying to steer the conversation away from Calvin's head. Yup. He was definitely hiding something. And Sara was going to find out what it was.

"It's a decent plan," said Sara. The curiosity was killing her and she was going to find out, one way or another. "I love your cap. Can I try it on?"

Calvin froze and then turned to his mother, who wagged her finger at him.

"Maybe later," he said. "After dinner or something." He took a bite of his food and avoided eye contact with Sara.

"That retirement plan…" said Gertrude. "Do you add extra each month or go with the minimum?"

Why the heck was this woman so obsessed with money? Especially if her son was worth millions? Did she really think Sara only set up this date to get at her son's cash? Sara had no idea Calvin even *had* money. His profile said he was in banking. It didn't say he owned the bank!

"I go with what they say," said Sara. "I have a new mortgage now, so I prefer to add extra to the principal payment each month if I'm going to spend some extra money on something."

"Of course. I bet it would be nice to have a husband who's well off. Then the pressure would be off to work so hard. Or you could stop working completely."

This woman was pathetic.

"Not really," Sara answered. "The kids can drive me crazy sometimes but I still love my job. It's rewarding and I don't have plans of giving up teaching anytime soon."

"Right," said Gertrude. "I've heard that one before."

Sara watched as Gertrude took a sip of her Chianti. The woman had a serious attitude.

"You want to come by the house after dinner?" asked Calvin. "Mom and I are going to watch *Fight Club*. You know, the one with Brad Pitt?"

Oh God.

Did he live with his mother? And did he really think that was an appropriate movie for a date?

"That's tempting but I need to get up early in the morning," she lied.

"I thought you were on summer vacation," said Gertrude.

"I...am. I...just moved into a new place and I want to paint one of the rooms." Sara looked at Calvin and pointed to his mother. "You two live together?"

Calvin nodded.

"Don't look so surprised," said Gertrude. "Kids in Europe live with their parents until they get married, sometimes well into their forties."

Sara choked on her Chianti again and Calvin promptly slapped her on the back like the last time. The waiter arrived with her food and Sara dove in. Ten minutes later the food was gone and she was satisfied. At least her stomach was satisfied. Her love life was another story.

She wiped her mouth and the napkin slipped out of her hand, falling to the floor.

Calvin bent down to pick up the napkin and the baseball cap fell off of his head.

"Oh Jesus Christ!" yelled Sara, staring at the top of Calvin's head. It was bandaged like he had a horrible accident. "Are you okay? What the hell happened to your head?"

Gertrude reached over and grabbed the cap from the floor and placed it gently back on her son's head. "That is *none* of your business."

"But his head is bandaged."

Calvin adjusted the cap. "Everything is fine."

Sara waited for him to continue but Calvin got back to his food.

Fine?

The guy's head looked like it got run over by a truck. Was he really not going to say anything at all? No explanation? This was too weird. Relationships were all about communication. Not that she was going to be having a relationship with Calvin, but still… You'd think he'd say *something*.

"Did you have an accident?" said Sara.

"No," said Calvin. "Nothing like that." He took another bite of food. "It's not as bad as it looks."

"You come from a poor family, don't you?" said Gertrude. "Admit it."

Sara had had enough. "No. I don't care about money."

"Well, you should."

Sara did a double take. This woman didn't make any sense at all.

Calvin held up his hand. "Mother, I'm going to tell her."

"It's not necessary."

"Yes, it is."

This should be good.

"I've had a few surgeries," he continued. "I have a rare skin disease and they had to remove part of my scalp. Fortunately they were able to pull excess skin from my bottom for the skin transplant."

"Your bottom?"

"Yeah..." Calvin pointed to his butt. "You know..."

What in the world?

Sara stared at Calvin's cap.

So they removed skin from his ass and stuck it on his head? Is this where the term "butthead" came from? Or maybe "asshat" fit better.

She felt bad for the guy, of course. But this seemed so bizarre.

Sara sighed. "Please excuse me. I think it's time for me to go." *Throw up.*

"Okay," said Gertrude. "But before you go I want to tell you I've made my decision. You can date my son."

Sara did another double take. Gertrude couldn't be serious.

"Yes!" said Calvin. "Can I call you, Sara?"

Unbelievable.

"No, thank you," said Sara, trying her best to stay calm. "And let me give you some advice. If you want any chance whatsoever of having sex in your adult life, you might want to leave your mother at home."

She turned and headed toward the front door and ran smack into the chest of her new neighbor. No mud this time. In fact, he was looking sharp in his designer jeans and black button-down shirt.

"I guess it was bound to happen," he said with a grin.

"What's that?" Sara asked, folding her arms across her

chest.

"You and me. Running into each other. We live in the same neighborhood and all of these great restaurants are within walking distance. Don't be surprised if we see each other every day."

She sighed. "Lucky me…"

"Look, we got off to a bad start and I think we should try again." He held out his hand. "I'm Ian."

Sara stared at his hand, wondering if this was a trick or something. Was he hiding one of those hand buzzers?

"Sara," she said, slowly accepting his hand.

He had amazing hands. Manly but smooth. He obviously used lotion. Very well-manicured too.

Ian grinned again. "You like what you see?"

"What are you talking about?"

"Nothing. But I was curious if you're going to give me back my hand anytime soon."

Sara dropped his hand like it was contaminated. "Oh! Sorry."

"Uh huh. I saw you when I came in." He pointed his head in the direction of Calvin and his mother. "Your husband and…mother-in-law?"

Sara chuckled. "Not even close."

"Your boyfriend with…his Aunt Betty?"

Sara laughed even harder but didn't answer. She really needed a laugh after that date.

Ian scratched his chin. "Mysterious. This isn't a date, is

it?"

"You ask a lot of questions."

"Just trying to get acquainted with my neighbor. I guess it's a date then. I can't figure out the older woman, though."

"There's nothing for you to figure out. I'm trying to make a graceful escape. Can you move out of my way please?"

"Of course." Ian stepped aside. "Dating's tough."

"Is it?"

Ian shrugged. "Meeting people. Pretending to be polite and sweet when all you really want to do is burp or spew out a few cuss words."

"Uh huh. You like to burp and cuss on dates?"

"No. I don't. But my point is you should be able to do that if you want. People are typically not themselves on dates and that can lead to problems down the road. You should always be yourself so everyone can really see what they're getting upfront. No surprises later that end in heartbreak or disappointment."

"Thank you for the advice, Dr. Phil."

"My pleasure. Feel free to cuss if it makes you feel better."

"Thanks for your permission and have a nice dinner."

"Or burp."

"I'm walking away."

"I'm going to pretend you're still here."

"You do that."

Sara walked past Ian and wanted to look back but resisted and continued out the front door. Was he eating alone? On a date? Was someone already waiting for him at a table? Ian was sexy but she wasn't sure about him. She knew she would be seeing more of him—nothing she could do about that. But if he woke her up tomorrow morning there would be hell to pay.

Chapter Three

"Please don't tell me…" Sara wiped her eyes and stared at the bedroom wall. The squealing noise had returned for an encore performance the next morning.
Ian had no idea who he was dealing with.

This time Sara didn't wait. She jumped up and banged on the wall three times, then regretted it. She knew what was going to happen. Her egotistical, stubborn neighbor was going to bang her back and then she would be even *more* pissed off. It would have been better to get up and knock on his door again. Of course, look how much good that did yesterday. He obviously hadn't taken her threats seriously. Not that she knew how to castrate a person but that was beside the point. She could have easily Googled it.

She knew what was coming. She stared at the wall and waited.

Bang! Bang! Bang! Bang!

Now we're at quadruple bangs? How dare he!

She slipped on her old Madonna t-shirt and khaki shorts and scratched Kili under her chin. "Come on, Kili. You need to pee and then we're going next door again. This time can you look a little more ferocious?"

Kili followed her out the front door and Sara wondered if there was a way to teach her to act more like Cujo and foam at the mouth. After Kili peed at the base of the birch tree Sara rang the doorbell and stared down at the new plant in the planter box.

She felt guilty. She wanted to replace the plant Kili had eaten but Ian beat her to it. A few seconds later the beautiful purple flowers and the rest of the new plant disappeared inside of Kili's mouth.

"No!" yelled Sara, pulling Kili back. Too late. The plant was gone. Again.

Ian opened the door. Shirtless.

That chest is kryptonite! And those abs! He's not playing fair!

She finally pried her gaze from the delicious nakedness of his upper body and made eye contact. Of course he was grinning.

He eyed her "Crazy for You" t-shirt. "You came to profess your love?"

She didn't answer.

Ian reached out to scratch Kili on the head. "How are you, girl? You're such a pretty thing—" He bent down to get a closer look at Kili's mouth and could see that she was chewing on something. He shot a look over at the empty planter box. "Do you ever feed her?"

"I…" She let out a deep breath. "I'm sorry, I owe you two plants now."

"I'll run a tab."

She pulled Kili away and headed back to her house. "Funny."

"Such a pleasure seeing you…"

"Yeah. A treat."

Sara closed the door behind her and realized she forgot to yell at Ian for waking her up.

Crap!

She wasn't going to go back there now. What was it with that guy? He flustered her and she couldn't focus in his presence. Of course Kili didn't help at all by eating his plants.

Sara went to the bathroom and splashed some water on her face, hoping to wash away the embarrassment. If only it were that easy.

She tried to focus on the day ahead of her. The next few hours would be dedicated to shopping to fill the empty fridge. The second half of the day would be used for emptying the final boxes from the move and going on another date.

After she returned from Mama Mia's last night she chatted with another potential male prospect, Buster. She laughed the first time she saw his name and wondered if it was a nickname. He confirmed he was named after Buster Keaton, a famous silent film actor from the early 1900s. But the name didn't matter. What mattered was him being a decent guy. And a great date.

*****

The day flew by and Sara had showered and was ready for her date with Buster. She had about ten minutes until his arrival so she took Kili out front for another pee.

She closed the front door behind her, looked up, and froze.

Ian was watching her summer dress dance with the wind. Did she just flash him? She used her free hand to hold the dress down against her thigh. Kili pulled toward Ian and licked his hand.

"Pink is one of my favorite colors," said Ian.

Crap.

She flashed him. He saw her pink panties.

Damn wind!

"Hello, Kili," continued Ian. He pet her on the head and she leaned into him, almost knocking him over. "How are you, you sweet thing? Can I speak to your mother or is she still crabby?"

Sara gave Ian the evil eye. "I will always be in a great mood as long as a certain neighbor doesn't wake me up early in the morning."

"Ahhh. So your happiness depends on others?"

Sara gave him another look. "We have to live next to each other so I suggest you get on my good side."

He glanced at her body and then made eye contact with Sara again. "Which side is your 'good' side?"

Sara hated when people made those air quotes. She pursed her lips but didn't answer.

"I see," said Ian, now stroking Kili on her side. "So if I don't get on your good side your dog will eat me?"

"She's a trained killer."

Kili clearly wasn't playing on the same team—all two hundred pounds of her plopped down on the ground in front of Ian and rolled over, requesting a little bit of love on the tummy and chest.

Ian laughed. "Yeah, I'm *really* scared."

What the heck was up with Kili and this guy? The dog was flirting with the neighbor, giving herself to him so easily like that. The slut.

"She's setting a trap," said Sara, pointing to her dog. "She makes it looks like she likes you and then when you let your guard down, bam! You're dinner."

Ian leaned down and rubbed Kili on the stomach. "This quite possibly is the sweetest dog I've ever met."

He was right, but Sara wasn't going to say anything. And she had to leave for her date with Buster. Time to get going.

"Okay, let's go Kili. Mommy needs to feed you before she goes on her—"

That was a close one. No need to tell Ian what she was up to, even though the nosy neighbor would probably find out on his own.

Ian eyed her dress again and raised an eyebrow. "Date?"

Sara froze. No hiding anything from this guy. And how

was she supposed to answer that?

Yes, I'm on my way to a very hot date. What's it to you?

Why would he ask her that anyway? She wondered if the man was single. Yeah, he was handsome. Okay, hot. But something weird was going on inside of that house of his. Who knew if he was a Unabomber? Or maybe he was operating a meth lab.

Sara pulled the leash and Kili jumped up. "I'm not going to answer that."

"That's a yes then. Hey, nothing wrong with going out. It's not easy to meet people, you know? It's tough out there."

Odd. That was the second time he'd said that.

"Right. Anyway, I hope that Kili doesn't make any noise while I'm gone. This place is new to her so she might get a little nervous when she hears noises. Especially weird noises coming from the neighbor."

"I have no idea what you're talking about."

"Of course you don't. Goodbye."

Ian grinned. "Goodbye."

Sara pulled Kili toward the house. She had a feeling that Ian was watching them and she wanted to turn back and look.

Don't! Go inside!

Sara had no willpower—she couldn't help herself. She turned around and looked back toward Ian's front door. Her sexy neighbor grinned and waved. She shook her head, went inside, and unclipped the leash from Kili.

"Smooth move," she said to herself. "Now he thinks you like him."

There was something about the guy that was appealing, besides his good looks and amazing chest and abs. He had a certain energy and if she wasn't mistaken, they had a little bit of a playful connection. But there was no way in hell she was going to get involved with another neighbor. If things didn't work out she would have to be reminded of it every single day she saw him. No way. Not gonna happen again.

Sara fed Kili and waited for Buster to arrive. Five minutes later the doorbell rang and she peeked out the window. A seven series BMW sat on the street and at the door was an overdressed man. Buster was about six feet tall with short, spiked black hair and a goatee. It was odd that he sported a suit considering they agreed on going to Aquí, a casual California-Mexican-fusion type restaurant well known in the area. Maybe he came straight from work.

Sara opened the door and smiled. "Hi, Buster."

Buster handed Sara a giant bunch of flowers and kissed her on the cheek. "Hi, Sara. You look beautiful."

Sara blushed. "Thank you." She stuck her nose in the flowers. "They smell amazing."

"They're called Lily of the Valley. Very expensive."

"Okay…"

Odd that he would tell her that. Was he trying to impress her by implying that he had money? It was already obvious by the car he was driving, but hopefully he wasn't one of those materialistic guys.

Okay, blow it off. Don't overanalyze things. Go out and have a good time.

Besides, they were off to a great start. He was polite and even brought her flowers.

Expensive flowers.

She held back the laughter and pushed Kili back, placing the flowers on the entryway table. She was starving so she'd put them in water when they got back since they wouldn't be gone very long.

"Okay, let's go."

Buster pointed to the flowers inside. "You aren't going to put those in water?"

Sara looked back at the flowers and then back to Buster. "Oh, I can do it when we get back. They'll be fine."

"Better to do it now. I'd hate to see anything happen to them. They're *very* expensive."

"Yes, you mentioned that earlier."

Buster looked serious but didn't say anything else.

"Okay," said Sara. "Give me a minute."

"Of course."

Sara pushed back inside the house and to the kitchen—the giant four-legged creature glued to her side. She sighed as she filled a vase with water and placed the flowers inside. "These are *very* expensive," she said to Kili. She smelled them again and smiled.

She wouldn't feel so bad if Kili ate these just to see the

reaction on Buster's face.

Maybe not such a good idea.

She placed the vase in the middle of the kitchen counter out of Kili's reach and went back outside to Buster. "Okay, all done. We can walk to the restaurant from here. It's only five minutes."

Buster turned and pointed in the direction of his BMW. "I prefer to take my car."

Your expensive car? "Okay," said Sara.

She felt strange driving to a place that was less than five minutes away. She loved being outside and being active and it was a beautiful evening for a walk. It was good for the environment too, but she wasn't going to argue with the guy. He could have had an injury or something that made walking difficult.

Buster's car was beautiful and the leather smelled great. Five blocks and thirty seconds later they arrived at Aquí and went inside. After they ordered the food they found a table and waited with their buzzer.

Buster's eyes traveled around the restaurant. "Interesting place."

Sara loved the decor, the southwestern theme, and the lively colors. "This is one of the most popular places to eat in town. Love the menu and the atmosphere. And great prices for the quality of food you're getting."

"The restaurants I typically go to don't have prices on the menu."

"Did they run out of ink when they were printing them?" Sara laughed.

It was clear Buster didn't share her sense of humor since he sat there dead-faced.

He stared at her for a moment. "I prefer the whole white tablecloth experience, people waiting on me, that sort of thing. I've worked hard and I deserve the best."

Not a good sign. Sara enjoyed trying a fancy place every now and then, but for her the company was always more important than the food.

She cocked her head to the side. "You've never nibbled on something at the farmer's market or grabbed something to eat from a food truck?"

Buster's mouth was open; he looked as if he had been insulted. "I prefer fancy." He looked around the restaurant and his eyes stopped on the little girl laughing and coloring at the table across from them. "I like places where you typically don't see children. Elegant, you know?"

This guy seemed a little too uptight and serious. Sara hadn't gotten that impression from their exchanges online. It didn't make sense at all. When they had swapped messages he was a great conversationalist and so carefree. He was so serious now.

"I'm confused," said Sara. "You mentioned you liked the street-side cafes in Europe. Most of those places are very casual."

"When did I say that?"

Great. The guy had a serious memory problem too.

"Just this morning."

"Oh." Buster scratched the side of his face. "Look, I'll be honest with you—my assistant wrote that."

"Your—"

"I've been pretty busy trying to flip a house. Bought it for 450k, gutted and redid it, and now I'm going to sell it for two million. We're putting the final touches on the landscaping before the open house this weekend."

"What does that have to do with street-side cafes and your assistant?"

"I've got a thousand irons in the fire and I don't have time for the daily chit chat, you know? So my assistant answers my emails. Occasionally."

Sara blinked. "How occasionally?"

"Pretty much all the time."

So all of the email exchanges Sara had were with the assistant.

Oh God.

Who was this guy? He didn't even look embarrassed!

Sara was deep in thought for a few moments. "So when you said that you loved the picture of me on top of the Eiffel Tower, that wasn't really you?"

"If it makes you feel any better, I'm sure I would have liked the picture had I seen it."

"Unbelievable."

"What?"

"It's just, I don't know. How do you expect to get to know someone if you don't show an interest and actually take part in the conversation?"

"I'm conversing with you now."

And what a conversation! The guy was pathetic. She stared at the buzzer on the table.

Buzz please!

The buzzer went off and vibrated.

Sara jumped up. "Yes!" She wasn't going to wait for him to offer to get the food. "I can get our food."

"You must be hungry," he said.

"Starving," she lied.

What was up with all of the loser guys? Silicon Valley was loaded with men: technology geeks, app developers, venture capitalists, real estate moguls, so many to choose from. The numbers were in her favor but she certainly wasn't having any luck. The best thing to do would be to get through dinner and let Buster know that this wasn't going to work out. He must sense their incompatibility too and realize they had no future together.

Twenty minutes later they finished eating. They had barely spoken to each other except when Buster mentioned he had a vacation condo in Cabo San Lucas. He also happened to mention he had one in Maui and on the French Riviera. Nice or Cannes? She couldn't remember. At that point she was trying to drown out his conversation with thoughts of her favorite chocolate chip cookies.

Buster's company was excruciatingly painful but at least the food was good. Sara had offered to walk home but he insisted on driving again. After they arrived back he walked Sara to her front door.

"You were quiet this evening," he said. "Not a bad thing since there are other ways to communicate." He winked.

Not gonna happen! "Thank you but I—"

Before Sara could react Buster leaned in, pressing his lips against hers.

She pushed him away and wiped her mouth. "What are you doing?"

"It's a kiss—people do that at the end of a date. No big deal."

"It's a big deal because I didn't want you to kiss me. Not now. Not ever!"

Sara didn't mean to sound that harsh or yell, but the guy deserved it.

Disgusting.

Buster adjusted his collar. "You're saying that now, but once Buster busts a move…"

Great. The guy is talking about himself in third person.

"Look," said Sara. "This isn't going to—"

Buster leaned in and tried to kiss Sara again.

Sara face-palmed him and pushed him back. "Stop doing that!"

"Don't be such a prude!" he yelled.

Ian's door flew open and he was immediately in Buster's

face. "Is there a problem here?"

"No problem at all," said Buster, sticking his chest out. "We just had a date and I was kissing her goodnight. Mind your own business."

Ian grabbed Buster's wrist, squeezed it hard, and twisted it behind his back. "This *is* my business. Sara is a friend of mine and it's obvious she's not interested. Take a hike. Now."

Ian let go of Buster's wrist and pushed him in the direction of his car.

What a neighbor!

Buster massaged his wrist. "I'm not scared of you."

"You have ten seconds to leave."

Buster eyed Ian up and down and let out a nervous laugh. "Right…"

"Ten…"

"Whatever. She's not even worth my time." Buster shook his head and walked to his car.

After he drove away Ian turned to Sara. "You okay?"

Sara nodded. "Thank you. The nerve of that guy…"

"Yeah, be careful. It's just a suggestion but you might want to meet your potential male suitors somewhere else instead of having them pick you up here. At least if it doesn't work out or if the guy's a psycho he won't know where you live."

"I wanted to meet him at the restaurant but he insisted on picking me up."

"I'm not surprised—the guy's a jerk. Just be careful,

okay? You're a beautiful—"

Ian stopped mid-sentence.

What was he going to say? A beautiful woman? A beautiful example of someone who's an idiot?

Sara stared into Ian's eyes. She saw kindness and could feel her heart accelerate a little bit.

What was that?

She knew exactly what that was. Butterflies!

Come on! Don't you go and get feelings for this guy! He's not your knight in shining armor! He just told the guy to leave. He didn't save your life or anything!

Ian broke eye contact with Sara. "Be careful."

"I will. Thanks." Sara unlocked her front door and turned back to Ian. "Goodnight."

"Goodnight, Sara."

Sara entered her house and closed the door behind her. She leaned against the door and blew out a deep breath. Kili ran to greet Sara and licked her fingers as she stood there deep in thought.

Ian was right. That wasn't a smart move giving in to Buster and letting him pick her up at home. He seemed like a catch online but obviously her instincts were wrong. And it wasn't even him online. The guy was a jerk who thought he could have whatever he wanted. No more taking chances with these men.

Kili pushed Sara's hand, looking for some love.

Sara bent down and wrapped her arms around Kili, as

much as was physically possible. "Sorry, my love. Did you miss me?"

"Woof!"

"Of course you missed your mommy."

"Woof!"

"Okay, pipe down there. We don't want to disturb our new neighbor."

Our handsome and noble neighbor.

Sara smiled and thought of what Ian did. Obviously she misjudged the guy. He was kind and he had a heart. She froze and her heart rate sped up even more. She suddenly had the urge to invite Ian over for a beer.

Should I invite him over? It's the least I could do, right? Maybe we would become friends.

Before she could talk herself out of it she went next door and rang the bell. Just a quick beer and a thank you for saving her from that slime ball. Nothing more.

Chapter Four

Ian opened the door and was presented again with his beautiful neighbor, this time without her pony. Was it his imagination or was Sara getting lovelier with each time that he saw her?

"Everything okay?" he asked.

"Yes. Absolutely. Of course." Sara chewed on one of her fingernails. "I wanted to say thanks again. For what you did."

He smiled. "It was nothing."

"No. It was something. In fact, I wanted to invite you over for a beer. To say thank you. I mean, if you're thirsty and have nothing more important to do. Do you like beer? I've got beer. Orange juice too. And hummus. And some gummy bears. Oh wait, I ate all of those."

Ian glanced over to her front door. "Is this a trap so your dog can eat me when I enter?"

Sara smiled. "You and I both know she's harmless."

He looked over to her place again. "Sure. A beer sounds great."

Ian closed the door behind him and followed Sara inside her place. He had never been inside the other townhomes in the community, but it was almost the exact same layout.

Obviously Kili was ready to play. She charged Ian, knocking him into the love seat. Then the real licking began.

Ian laughed and stuck his hand out to pat her on her side. "Now that's what I call passion."

"Kili! Come here."

"It's okay, really. I don't mind at all."

Kili licked Ian and nudged his arm, asking for a stroke or two.

Sara covered her eyes. "I don't know what's gotten into her."

Ian really didn't mind the dog being so affectionate with him. Kili was a sweet thing.

"She's usually not this rough with strangers," said Sara.

Ian continued to laugh. "I may need a squeegee later for the slobber."

Sara laughed. "Cookie!"

Kili jumped off of Ian and turned to face Sara. She sat and panted, waiting.

"What a smart girl," said Ian.

"She has her moments. One thing I learned early on is that she's easily bribed."

"They must be special cookies."

"Nah—she's not that picky. Just rawhide, but she goes crazy for them. Any mischief she's into will immediately come to a halt when I say the magic word."

"Cool…"

Sara grabbed a rawhide treat from the container on top

of the fridge and held it up in the air. "Give me your paw."

Kili obeyed and held out her giant paw.

Sara grabbed it and shook it. "Good girl. Now the other."

Kili dropped one paw and held out the other paw for Sara to grab.

"Good girl. Down."

Kili plopped to the floor with a big thump and Sara rewarded her with the treat.

Sara smiled and turned to Ian. "You ready for your treat too?"

"Yeah, I'd love some rawhide beer."

"Sorry. All out. You'll have to settle for beer from Holland."

"Ahh! Even better. Sounds great."

Sara popped open two bottles of Heineken and they retreated to the living room to sit on the sofa. There were candles everywhere. Purple, red, orange. The place had a homey feel—she did a great job decorating and he wondered how she did it so fast, considering she just moved in.

Kili walked over and laid down on top of Ian's feet.

Sara nearly spit out her beer. "Kilimanjaro!"

Ian laughed. "That's a mouthful."

"That's why I only use her full name when she's getting into trouble or being bossy." Sara tilted her head and watched Kili close her eyes. "I think she has a crush on you or something. You seem to have some magical spell on her."

Uh oh. Kili must be responding to Billy's cologne. God, I hope not.

He reached down to stroke her along the length of her body. The dog was massive and he knew he wouldn't have any feeling in his feet in a matter of minutes.

"She's beautiful," said Ian. "And so sweet."

"Thanks. She's my baby." Sara crinkled her nose. "Okay, that sounded pathetic."

"Not at all. Dogs are amazing creatures." Ian held out his beer toward Sara. "To dogs."

Sara smiled and tapped his bottle with hers. "To dogs."

"And neighbors."

Sara laughed and toasted again. "And neighbors."

Ian took a sip of his beer and chuckled. "This is the first time I've actually been inside somebody's place here. Many of the people who live here work in high-tech and are on the job so much I barely see them. They go home and collapse every night."

"Like me sometimes."

Ian nodded. "What do you do?"

"I'm a teacher."

Ian was about to take another sip and paused.

"What?" asked Sara.

"Nothing. I'm a teacher too."

"Really?"

Ian nodded. "High school. I teach art."

"Huh…" She smiled. "I teach geography. Junior high."

"What a coincidence. Two teachers."

"And two neighbors…"

"We may have some other things in common."

"Like what?"

Ian shrugged. "I don't know. Ever been to prison?"

Sara blinked three times.

Ian laughed. "I'm kidding."

Sara let out a loud breath. "Not funny."

"Sorry. Okay, let me think about this for a second." He put his index finger on his temple and pretended to be deep in thought. "Here's one…have you ever been on top of the Eiffel Tower?"

Sara analyzed Ian for a moment and then glanced back to her fireplace mantel where a statue of the Eiffel Tower was prominently displayed. "Ahhhh." She shook her finger at Ian. "Nice try. Cheater."

"What?"

Sara pointed to the statue.

"Oh, wow! Is that the Eiffel Tower?"

"No. It's the Campbell water tower. Of course it's the Eiffel Tower! You saw it."

Ian laughed and took a sip of his beer. "I never noticed it."

"Uh huh…"

"I studied in Paris for a year and have a minor in French. I *love* France."

"Me too."

"Another thing we have in common!"

Sara laughed and took a sip of her beer. "So I guess that means you're fluent?"

"Oui oui."

He took another sip and admired his beautiful new neighbor. She wasn't as uptight as he thought when he first met her. She had some personality and he could see the playful side of her. That playful side made her more attractive. Sexier.

"Do you like pizza?" asked Ian.

"Very much."

"There's something else!"

He held out his bottle to clink hers and she stared at it.

Sara squished her eyebrows together. "*Every*body loves pizza."

"No. Not everybody. My aunt Marmaduke doesn't."

"Right. You expect me to believe that—" Sara furled her eyebrows. "Wait a minute. You have an aunt named Marmaduke?"

"Yeah. Why? Do you know her?"

Sara laughed. "Marmaduke?"

"Yes! Marmaduke!"

Sara stared at Ian. "Huh…"

Ian couldn't hold it in any longer and burst out with laughter.

"Oh!" said Sara. "Okay, you got me good."

Ian took a sip of his beer and smiled. "Yes, I did."

Right there. What was that?

Sara and Ian had a moment.

A moment where they connected. A moment where it felt like they had known each other for years. A moment where he was so tempted to move closer and kiss her. But where the hell did that come from? They barely even knew each other. Ian had heard hundreds of stories about love at first sight and all that mumbo jumbo. Could people really connect with each other so quickly? Maybe it was the beer.

Yeah. Definitely the beer. But he had only had a few sips so he wasn't even close to drunk.

Sara pointed at Ian's head. "What were you thinking there?"

"Where?"

She leaned over and lightly tapped the side of his head. "There."

"Nothing."

"Uh huh."

She looked like she was analyzing Ian again. She must have felt something too; it was quiet in the room.

Ian needed a distraction.

He reached over and ran his fingers across the surface of her globe on the table next to the sofa. All of the countries were made of gemstones. "Cool globe."

"Thanks."

He spun the globe and let his finger hover over it as it rotated around and around. "Wherever my finger lands, you'll be going there on a vacation soon."

"Are you some kind of psychic, fortune teller, globe spinner?"

"Shhh. I'm concentrating here."

Sara laughed. "So sorry. Please, carry on…"

He let his finger drop, the pressure stopping the globe.

Sara stood up and leaned over to see where his finger landed. "Based on your finger, I will be going on a trip to Cuba."

"Hasta la vista, baby."

Sara shook her head. "That could be a fascinating trip but there are a hundred other places I would much rather visit first. I've got a list."

"Add Cuba to the top."

"I don't think so. And what would I do there anyway?"

"Well, it's an island, as you know. So…go to the beach. Don't forget to pack your bikini."

"What makes you think I wear a bikini? I may be a conservative one-piece gal."

Ian eyed her body. "No way. Wearing a one-piece with a body like yours would be like slapping Mother Nature in the face."

Sara opened her mouth and then closed it. She took a sip of her beer and analyzed the label on the bottle. She looked like she was avoiding eye contact with him.

What the heck did he say that for? Yes, it was the truth—he'd noticed her body before. Nothing wrong with that. She had a beautiful body and people would naturally be aware of it.

Sara was staring at him. Did she feel disrespected? Or was she shy? He couldn't get a read on her.

"I need to ask you something," said Sara.

"Yes, I wear a one-piece."

Sara laughed. "Good to know."

"Go for it," said Ian. "What's your question?"

"What's that weird noise always coming from your place?"

Ian took another sip of his beer. "Ahhh. That."

He thought about it for a moment. Should he tell her? Maybe she would think it was silly. Or worse, she would ask to see it. The lighthouse was in no condition to be seen. In fact, he was going to scrap it and start all over again. He didn't like the perfectionist in himself. He considered it his biggest flaw. Things don't always have to be perfect. And ninety-nine point nine percent of the world wouldn't even notice the imperfections in the tower. But the problem was *he* would notice. His father would notice.

"Just something I'm working on," he finally answered.

"Oh, okay," said Sara. "You don't have to share."

"Sorry." He must have looked like an idiot. This kind woman was asking a simple question and he couldn't even give her a simple answer?

Tell her. "The noise comes from a potter's wheel."

"A potter's wheel…"

She seemed to be taking in the information.

"Yeah," said Ian. "I'm making a present for my grandparents."

"Really?"

Ian nodded. "A lighthouse, to be exact."

Sara smiled. "I *love* lighthouses. Whenever I take Kili over to the beach in Santa Cruz we always walk by the lighthouse there."

Ian loved Sara's smile. It was like lightning—a force of positive energy that reached out and zapped everything in its path. And it loosened up Ian enough to share a little more.

"The one I'm replicating—I should say *trying* to replicate—is the Piedras Blancas lighthouse down in San Simeon. It was built in 1875."

"I haven't seen that one but I bet it's beautiful. Why did you choose that particular lighthouse to build? Did you grow up over there?"

"No. My grandfather proposed to my grandmother at the base of that lighthouse and they're going to celebrate their fiftieth wedding anniversary soon. I thought it would be a nice gift."

"Nice?" asked Sara.

"Yeah. You don't think so?"

Ian saw her eyes tear up.

"It's more than nice," she continued. "It's beautiful and so sweet."

"I still need to finish it, which is proving to be quite the task. I can't get it the way I want it. There was an impressive replica of the same lighthouse at a gallery not too far from San Simeon. In Cambria. It would have been a lot easier to buy that one instead of trying to do it myself."

Sara shook her head. "You're doing the right thing. This is more unique."

Ian couldn't argue with that. The thought of his grandparents receiving the present made him happy.

"You're smiling," said Sara. "What were you thinking?"

"You're right. Of course it would be much more unique if I made it." He took a sip of his beer. "There was a time when I wanted to open my own gallery."

"What stopped you?"

"Teaching is the safer route. At least that's what my dad had drilled into my head. But after talking with that gallery owner in Cambria the feelings of having my own gallery returned."

"Sometimes you just have to go for what you want."

There was that smile of hers again. Beautiful. She kept her eyes on Ian and took a sip of her beer. He took a sip and kept eye contact with her.

Are we thinking the same thing? She mentioned going for it but she was talking about the gallery, right?

There it was again, that feeling. And it was coming from her. They were connecting again.

I love that feeling.

Ian put his hand to his chest and could feel the thumping.

"What?" asked Sara.

"Nothing," he answered. He reached down to pet Kili who was still laying directly on top of his feet. "You have the coolest dog."

"That was smooth the way you changed subjects, but I agree with you. And just a warning, you're going to lose the circulation in your feet soon."

Ian grinned. "It already happened. I'd hate to disturb her though—she looks so peaceful."

"Don't worry about her—she has plenty of time to sleep. I'll get her to move." Sara stood up and went toward the fridge. Kili lifted her head to see what Sara was doing.

"Gonna bribe her with another cookie?" asked Ian.

Kili jumped up and slammed into Ian, knocking the beer bottle out of his hand. She wedged her way out of the small space, pushing the coffee table to the side like it was made of cardboard. She ran to Sara and sat obediently in front of her, waiting.

"Oh God," said Sara, dropping the treat on the floor for Kili and rushing over to Ian with a kitchen towel. "I'm so sorry. You need to be careful with that word."

Ian stood up and set the empty beer bottle on the coffee table. His shirt and pants were soaked.

Sara dabbed the towel into his chest, trying to soak up the beer. "I'm really sorry about this. I'll buy you a new shirt."

"Is that before or after you buy me two new plants?"

Sara chuckled and glanced at his lips for a moment and then turned her attention back to his shirt. She was doing a lot of dabbing and he kind of enjoyed it. His heart rate kicked up a few beats per second.

Take your time.

Ian felt the temperature in the room spike upwards when he looked at her lips. Literally every second that went by she was more beautiful. He wanted to kiss her right there but that was crazy. And he was sure he would be greeted with a slap in the face or a kick to the balls. What was he thinking? He just met her. There was something about this woman. They were silent, but he was so curious about what she was thinking. She looked a little nervous as she dried his shirt. Was she reading his mind!

I hope not!

Her gaze lifted to his lips, but she quickly turned her attention back to his shirt. She moved the towel lower toward his pants and he grabbed it from her hands.

"Yeah," he said. "I can take over from here. Thank you."

"Good idea…"

That was an interesting moment. They had a connection all right, he could feel it. Out of nowhere.

He looked down at his clothes again. "I should go change out of this."

"Okay. See you back here in a few?"

He wanted to return but he also knew he needed to get back to his project. He looked up at the clock on the wall.

"It's getting late."

Sara nodded. "Of course." She walked him to the door and Kili followed them. "Thanks again for what you did earlier. That was kind of you." Kili licked Ian's hand and Sara smiled. "Looks like Kili wanted to thank you too."

"My pleasure. Anytime." Ian scratched Kili on the head and then made eye contact with Sara. "Good night. Thanks for the beer."

"Ha! Your clothes should thank me for it."

He grinned. "There's always another time."

Sara pointed back inside her place. "You know where I live."

Ian laughed. "That I do. Hey, are you going to the festival tomorrow?"

"What festival?"

Ian laughed. "Okay, I guess that would be a *no*."

"Not necessarily. Tell me about it and then I'll decide if I'm going or not."

"We have lots of festivals here in the downtown area," he said. "They shut down the street and everything. Tomorrow is the first one of the summer and it's an evening art and wine festival. It goes from four until nine."

"Oooh, sounds like fun."

"It is. There's entertainment and—"

"Art and wine?"

Ian chuckled. "You're a wise woman."

"Thanks for noticing. I guess I'll see you there. Sorry

again for…you know." She pointed to his wet shirt. "*That.* Kili's sorry too."

Ian laughed. "No worries. Goodnight."

"Goodnight."

She shut the door and Ian stood there staring at it.

Was this a date?

He wasn't sure. But it sure as hell felt like a date.

Chapter Five

Sara took forever to get ready for the art & wine festival the next day. Ten different outfits were sprawled across the bed. *This is ridiculous.*

She sighed. "This isn't a date, so why are you so nervous?"

Kili lifted her head at the sound of her mother's voice.

"Your mother has issues and likes to talk to herself. Don't judge me. I'm the one that puts food on the table. Or...in your bowl."

Kili blew out a deep breath and laid her head back down on the floor.

Sara scanned the clothes on the bed. "Seriously, just pick something."

She finally grabbed the teal blouse that would match her new Franco Sarto shoes and slipped on a white skirt. A couple of turns in the mirror and she was set. She fed Kili and walked to the festival.

Sara was looking forward to seeing Ian again. The guy had a stable job, wasn't too weird, and was good-looking. A sense of humor too. But she was fooling herself if she thought something was going to happen between them.

"Friends," she said. "Nothing more. You can't have too many friends."

She contemplated a friends scenario with Ian as she walked across the trolley tracks and by Blue Line Pizza into downtown Campbell.

Can I really be friends with someone who's that good-looking?

Sara wanted more. Yes, she needed to find a date for Tiffany's wedding but what she really longed for was a steady man in her life. A good man who was fun and normal. One who didn't play games and one who was committed.

All in.

Sara stopped at the first booth, where a necklace seemed to be calling her name. She waved at the woman selling the hand-made jewelry.

"It looked like something caught your eye," said the woman.

Sara smiled. "That one." She pointed to the necklace.

"Great choice," said the woman, removing the necklace from the display. "It's sterling silver with a beautiful turquoise stone. Try it on." She handed Sara the necklace and slid the mirror over on the table in front of her so she could see herself.

Sara wrapped the necklace around her neck and felt for the clasp.

"I can help you with that," said a sexy voice behind her.

Ian.

"Oh…" said Sara. "Thank you."

Before she could turn around Ian took the ends of the necklace from her, brushing her hands with his in the process. His touch was like a little jolt to her system. She took a deep breath—all of a sudden it was a little harder to breathe. She rubbed her palms together. Sweat.

How could he have this effect on her? All he was doing was helping with the necklace!

Sara could feel his breath on the back of her neck and it took all of her willpower to focus on something else. Damn, she was enjoying it! So much that she pressed her hand to her stomach as the butterflies started salsa dancing.

She peeked into the mirror and could see Ian standing behind her in a navy blue polo shirt, his dark blond hair sticking up all over the place and sexy as hell. He was focused on the clasp, but Sara watched Ian inch a little closer to take in her scent.

He grinned that sexy grin. "You smell amazing."

"Thanks. I shower regularly."

God! Where the hell did that come from? Why am I so nervous?

Ian chuckled. "We all appreciate that very much."

Sara's thoughts were all over the place and Ian was taking forever to put on the necklace! *He was helping—that's all.* She was enjoying his touch, but now the woman was staring at her.

"Is there a problem?" asked the woman.

"It's just…" said Ian. "Hmm. Yeah, I guess there is. It doesn't seem to want to attach to the other end."

"Let me take a look."

Ian handed the necklace to the woman and he turned to Sara. "Glad you made it."

"Me too," said Sara.

"How's Kili today?"

"She's great, although she was acting a little weird before I left the house to come here."

"How so?"

"I took her out front for a pee and after she was done she pulled me to your front door. Then she got up on her hind legs against your door and barked. Almost as if she was calling for you to come out."

Ian opened his mouth and then closed it. His cheeks reddened.

"What?" asked Sara.

"Nothing. That's odd."

Ian broke eye contact with Sara and looked down the street.

That's weird. He has a guilty look on his face.

"Here," said the woman, holding out the necklace.

Sara stepped forward and swung around. The woman clasped the necklace around her neck without a problem.

"Must be child-proof," said Sara, laughing.

Ian chuckled. "Must be…"

"What do you think?" interrupted the woman.

Sara looked at herself in the mirror and smiled. "I like it." She turned to Ian. "What do you think, neighbor?"

"Beautiful," he said.

Ian wasn't looking at the necklace. He was looking directly into her eyes when he said that.

She felt her heart rate accelerate and turned back to the woman. "How much is it?"

"Seventy-five."

Sara smiled. "I'll take it."

"Great," said the woman. "Would you like to see the matching bracelet?"

"Oh…" said Sara, searching the display. "I didn't know there was one."

"Yes. I made them both the same day. It's the same price as the necklace."

The woman pulled the bracelet from the case and handed it to Sara.

"Wow," said Sara, wrapping it around her wrist. "It's beautiful." She held her hand out in front of her and admired it a little more. "Hmmm. Let me think about this one, if you don't mind. I just got here and there's still so much to see." She removed the bracelet and handed it back to the woman.

"Of course," said the woman. "I'll be here all evening."

"Great."

Sara pulled her wallet out of her purse and handed the woman four twenties for the necklace.

The woman smiled and handed Sara a five dollar bill back. "Thank you."

Ian pointed to the street in front of them, lined on both sides with arts and crafts booths, as well as food and wine stations. "There's lots to see."

"I can't wait." She eyed the next booth. "Do you always come to the festivals?"

Ian nodded. "As much as I can—I love them. It's a chance to get out, get some fresh air, and also support the locals. Campbell is known for their community events and I know a lot of the people here. For instance, that guy over there." Ian pointed to a man standing underneath a canopy full of paintings. "I went to college with him and he's one of the other art teachers in my department."

Before Sara could say something the man yelled. "Ian! Come over here and buy my paintings."

Ian laughed. "You give me one every year for Christmas. Why start buying them now?"

They approached the smiling man, who eyed Sara. "Who's the lovely lady?"

She smiled and held out her hand. "I'm Sara."

He accepted her hand. "Michael." Then he pointed to Ian. "Is this a date?"

Sara jerked her head back, surprised by the question. She turned to Ian to check out his body language and to see how he would respond. *Does Ian think they were on a date?*

"We're neighbors," said Ian. "She moved in next door over the weekend."

Okay, so he didn't think it was a date. Fine. But he's single and has no girlfriend otherwise Michael would know.

Why did Sara feel disappointed? She shouldn't because she didn't date neighbors anymore. And technically, when Ian mentioned the festival he asked her if she was going. He never asked her to go *with* him.

"Really…" said Michael, shifting his head back and forth between Ian and Sara. "Looks like a date to me."

"Okay," said Ian, putting his arm around Sara, making her jump. "You caught us—it's actually much more than that. In fact, we're engaged to be married."

Michael's eyes darted back and forth between Sara and Ian. "Now *that* I don't believe."

"Seriously," said Ian. He smiled and turned toward Sara. "Isn't that right, honeybunch?"

Sara smiled. She didn't mind at all playing this game. One of her favorite things as a child was to play make-believe. Besides, his arm felt wonderful around her shoulder.

"Absolutely, my honeysuckle Rose," she said. "And I can't wait for our honeymoon in Greece. I love the nude beaches."

Michael's mouth was open. So was Ian's.

Ian swallowed hard. "I could use a drink. Would you like a glass of wine?"

Sara smiled. "I'd love one."

They said goodbye to Michael and walked toward the wine booth to buy tickets for the wine.

Sara eyed her shoulder—there was still an arm attached to it. "Are we still playing make-believe?"

"Oh…" Ian let out a nervous laugh and removed his arm from around her. "Sorry."

Sara giggled. "That was fun."

"You're good at it. Let me know when you'd like to play again."

"You want to be my pretend boyfriend at a wedding? That would solve a lot of my problems."

Oops. Didn't mean to say that out loud.

Ian turned to her. "What do you mean?"

"Nothing."

"You looking for a date to a wedding? I'm in."

So tempting.

"Thanks, but I don't date my neighbors," she said.

"Who said it was a date? We would be pretending, remember?"

She tried to distract him and pointed to a wine station. "Wine!"

No way would she take him to the wedding. She had fun pretending with him. But she could see how too much pretending would start to feel real. Not gonna happen.

They got their first glass of wine and turned to each other.

Ian raised his glass to Sara for a toast. "To *not* spilling anything on myself."

Sara laughed. "Cheers. And that shouldn't be a problem since Kili's not here."

"True, but you never know…"

Sara took a sip of her wine and smiled. She liked Ian. Especially when he was behaving and not waking her up at the crack of dawn.

"Welcome, everyone," boomed the voice from the main stage. "Are you ready to dance?"

A few people clapped and yelled, but most of the attendees were just getting there.

The band started playing their version of "Respect" by Aretha Franklin.

"Fun," said Sara. "I love this song."

Ian pointed to the dance floor. "Then we should dance."

Sara's heart rate sped up.

Definitely feels like a date.

But then she thought back to what he said earlier.

We're neighbors.

But her neighbor was asking her to dance. And the dance floor was a ghost town, not a single person making their way to dance.

"Really?" asked Sara. "You're joking, right?"

Hopefully he was joking. She wouldn't mind dancing with him, but—

"You said you like the song."

"I do."

"Then?"

Sara shrugged.

"You don't like to dance?" he asked.

"Yeah, but…"

"Well...?"

She shrugged again. "It's just that..." She pointed to the dance area. "How about if we wait until more people are out there dancing?"

He laughed. "You're scared people will be staring at us?"

"Well...yeah."

"You don't want to be seen with me?"

"No. I mean, yes! I mean...I have no problem being seen with you. But yes, I guess I'm a little self-conscious."

"Take my hand."

She stared at his hand and smiled. "Why?"

"Take it."

"No."

Ian took a sip of his wine. "Okay, tell me this—have you ever been scared of something, really scared, but then after you did it you were like, 'Man, I wish I would've done this earlier'?"

"Yes, of course."

Ian surveyed the area. "This is one of those times. And the song is going to end if you don't hurry."

She let out a deep breath and stared at the big empty dance floor. "I may need some liquid courage."

"Great idea. On the count of three we slam our glasses of wine. Ready?"

She stared at her glass. "The entire thing? No way."

"One."

"I'm not going to do it."

"Two."

"This is ridiculous, people don't slam wine. It's meant to be sipped."

"Live a little. Three!"

Sara didn't know what possessed her but she did it. In just a few seconds she drank her entire glass of wine. She was also not sure why she screamed with joy and gave Ian a high-five. She's not a high-five kind of person! But she did it.

Ian laughed. "See? You stepped out of your comfort zone. Good. Now dance with me."

"Okay."

They set their empty glasses down on a table near the stage and headed to the middle of the dance floor. Then the music stopped.

"Crap," said Sara.

"Don't worry. They'll play another song. Nobody is paying attention to us at all. We are invisible."

"Well, look over here!" boomed the voice of the lead singer from the stage. "Our first dancers of the evening!"

Sara would need a calculator to count the heads that turned in their direction, but she knew the percentage: One hundred percent.

She felt her face heat up and could feel her pulse in her neck. "Okay, we lost our chance to dance. Let's get something to eat."

She made a move back toward their empty wine glasses.

Ian grabbed her hand before she could escape. "Not so

fast. I have a sneaking suspicion they are going to play more than one song this evening."

"Let's play a slow song for the two lovebirds this evening," said the lead singer of the band. "The rest of you, feel free to join in."

Lovebirds?

Ian still held her hand and spun her around a few times. "This is fun."

"Says who? If I had any cookies I would be tossing them."

Ian frowned. "Sorry. I guess I'm a little too eager to dance with you."

Sara felt bad. The guy was being a total gentleman and just wanted to dance with her. Why was she so uptight?

Loosen up. Please!

The band jumped into "Let's Get it On" by Marvin Gaye.

Ian grabbed Sara's other hand. "Great song."

Sara's shoulders suddenly loosened up. And she closed her eyes and took a deep breath as Ian pulled her closer.

He smelled good. He *felt* good.

She felt a little smile coming on as Ian pulled away to look at her face.

"See? It's not so bad, is it?"

"No."

A few other couples joined them on the dance floor. All eyes wouldn't be just on them anymore. Although she had to admit for the last thirty seconds or so, she completely forgot about the people around her. In fact, there were moments when she didn't even hear the music. Just the sound of his heart against her cheek. It felt good. She had missed these moments, simple moments, really. Living in the present. Enjoying the company of another person. Chemistry.

Ian moaned and it caught her off guard. Oh wait, that was Sara who moaned.

Crap.

Ian pulled away to look into her eyes. "There's something very cool about you…"

"Thank you."

"…when you're not so crabby."

Sara removed her hand from around his neck and pinched his side. "I'm *not* crabby."

He laughed. "Sorry. Okay, okay." He smiled and maintained eye contact with her. "Let me make it up to you by telling you something else."

She held up her index finger and thumb and tapped them together. "Go ahead. But I've got these two babies on standby. Don't make me pinch again."

Ian let go of her hand and ran his fingers through some of the hair that was hanging over her ear. "I…love your hair. So soft."

Yes! That softening conditioner really works! Am I drunk already?

He let go of her hair and grabbed her hand again. He caressed the outside of her hand with his thumb.

Ooh, I like that.

Yup, she was feeling something now. She realized she had dropped her gaze to his lips and was staring.

She tried to distract him and looked over toward the table where they had left their empty wine glasses. They needed them for refills. "Are you thirsty? I'm thirsty. Good—nobody stole our glasses."

When Ian didn't answer she slowly turned back to him to get a read on his face. The guy was grinning.

Guess he didn't fall for that. Nice mouth. I bet his lips are soft. As soft as my hair. But I doubt he uses lip softening conditioner. Is there such a thing? Is he going to kiss me? I can't tell. But oh how I would love that. Damn, I'm so impatient. And definitely tipsy too. I may regret this.

Sara reached up and kissed Ian on the lips.

Her head told her to pull away but her heart was telling her to pull him closer. What was he going to think of her? You don't just go around kissing people on the street. In some countries that was illegal! What if he didn't want to kiss her or didn't like her kiss?

That wasn't going to be an issue. Ian moaned and pulled Sara closer, deepening the kiss. If he wasn't enjoying it he would push her away or throw up on her. No, this was the opposite. The man was in charge now and he definitely knew what he was doing.

Would it be wrong to rip his clothes off right here?

Sara pulled away and forced a smile. She stepped back,

needing space. Her fingers covered her lips. If kissing was an Olympic sport Ian would be stepping up to the platform to receive his gold medal.

Now would come that awkward moment. Someone needed to say something. Anything. And would one of them say that amazing kiss was a mistake? Hopefully not. And who would say something first? Knowing how nervous she got, it would be her.

"I love food," she blurted out.

That was pathetic.

Ian burst out in laughter. "I guess that means you prefer to not talk about what happened." He pointed to a food station with Polish dogs. "You want one?"

"Sounds great."

Truth be told, Sara had never experienced a kiss like that. Ever. Her legs were still a little wobbly and it wasn't from the wine.

They grabbed their wine glasses and headed to the food booth. Sara could see a man behind the booth barbecuing the Polish dogs that smelled so amazing. Her eyes followed the clouds of smoke into the sky, still deep in thought over that kiss.

"He told me he needed space," said a female voice behind Ian and Sara. "He wasn't ready for something so serious."

"So typical," said another female voice behind them.

That little exchange reminded Sara of the last

conversation she had with her ex, Brian, before they broke up. He said the exact same thing. But the worst part was her ex lived right next door and she had to continue to see him after the breakup. And being neighbors with your ex is one of the worst things ever. She finally couldn't take it anymore and moved ten miles, from South San Jose to Campbell. It wasn't a huge distance, but enough to make sure she didn't see him every single day.

She casually glanced over to Ian. Her next door neighbor.

What am I doing?

There was no way she wanted to go through that drama again. Plus, she loved her new townhome. What if she had to move again because things didn't work out after getting involved with Ian?

No way. The kiss was amazing and she liked Ian, but this was not going to happen. They would finish their meal and she would excuse herself.

Just friends.

She had to be strong. Any thoughts of that kiss and that dance would place doubts in her head. And doubts were the enemy.

"Hi, Miss Larson!"

Sara jumped and swung around. She smiled at her co-worker, Becky Frasier, hugging her.

Becky—more commonly known as Miss Frasier—taught history at Sara's school. They were friends but both were so busy lately they barely had a chance to hang out. In fact, they hadn't talked in over three weeks. Sara introduced her to Ian.

"Another teacher?" said Ian.

Becky nodded. "The proud. The underpaid. The underappreciated."

Ian chuckled and pointed to the menu board above their heads. "You want a Polish dog?"

"Sounds great."

Ian waved away her money when she opened her purse. "I've got it. How about you two grab a table since they're disappearing? I'll be right there with the food and all of the fixings."

Sara squeezed Ian's arm and smiled. "Thanks. That sounds great."

Firm biceps—gotta love it. Quit touching him! Friends!

Sara and Becky sat at one of the tables and looked back at the line where Ian was ordering the food.

Becky jumped in. "He's handsome."

Sara turned back to Becky. "He's my neighbor."

"Is that all? Just a neighbor?"

Sara let out a big breath. "Yes. Why?"

"I mean I saw something between you two happening out there on the dance floor a few minutes ago."

"Oh…"

"That was no ordinary dance and it certainly was no ordinary kiss."

She got that right. In fact Sara was a little disappointed that the Polish dog would remove the taste of Ian from her mouth. Maybe she didn't have to eat. Or maybe she needed another one of those kisses later.

Stop it! Control your thoughts!

She glanced back to the food station where Ian was getting napkins.

Nice butt, neighbor.

She wanted to kill her brain. She had no willpower.

"We're friends," said Sara. "The kiss was a mistake brought on by the wine."

"Really?"

"Really."

Ian arrived at the table with the Polish dogs, napkins, and condiments. "Here we go." He passed Sara and Becky their food and sat across from them. Sara could feel Ian's analyzing eyes looking at her and Becky.

He knows we've been talking. Must be our body language. Act natural!

"Everything okay?" asked Ian.

"Great!" said Becky, with a little too much enthusiasm. "Thanks for this."

Ian studied them both again. "I have a feeling that I missed something important. I assume you had some girl-talk while I was gone but—"

"Love this!" said Sara, chewing her first bite. She hoped that would be enough to change the subject.

Ian laughed and held out some packets of ketchup and mustard. "You don't need any?"

She shook her head and continued to chew.

Ian stuck the end of the packet of ketchup in his mouth and tore it open. He added some on top of his sausage and took a bite. The force of his bite shot the dog out of the other end of the bun and it landed on the bottom of his shirt.

"Okay," he said. "I've forgotten how to eat food." He grabbed the dog, stuck it back in the bun, and placed it on top of a napkin on the table. Then he stared down at his shirt.

Becky dipped her napkin in her white wine and jumped up. "Let me help." She lifted his shirt enough to expose his sexy midsection and started trying to remove the mess with her napkin.

Well, hello there! Check out those abs.

Ian must have noticed Sara staring.

He pulled his shirt down and forced a smile. "It's okay, Becky. Thanks for your help, but I'm going to run and get cleaned up. I shall return shortly."

Becky smiled. "I look forward to it."

She looks forward to what? His return?

Becky sat back down and smiled, taking a bite of her bun.

Oh God. Becky has the hots for Ian.

Sara continued and after a few more bites, the Polish dog

disappeared. She wiped her mouth and stood up. The more she thought about it, the more she knew that having anything to do with Ian would be a mistake. She couldn't take a chance.

Becky looked up at Sara with curiosity. "Bathroom?"

Sara shook her head. "I realized I forgot to feed Kili. Can you tell Ian I had to go home? And tell him thanks for everything."

"Will do. You coming back?"

Sara was hoping she wouldn't ask. She hadn't planned on returning.

"I'll try," she lied.

She walked home, mentally scolding herself for what she had done. It was a bad idea to go to the festival. But she did the right thing leaving—she kept telling herself. She and Ian shared a wonderful dance and an amazing kiss. Better to cut things off now before they got awkward.

Hopefully it wasn't too late.

Chapter Six

Ian headed out for a morning walk on the Los Gatos Creek Trail. He passed the basketball courts in Campbell Park and entered the trail, walking toward the percolation ponds.

He hoped some fresh air would clear his mind and help him figure out what happened yesterday with Sara. He couldn't understand why she had left the festival without saying goodbye. That dance and that kiss rocked his world. He wasn't an expert on women—no man was—but he could at least tell that she was enjoying herself. That's what made her sudden departure even more puzzling.

Two bicyclists rode in Ian's direction, side-by-side, and he stepped off the path to let them pass with ease. A flock of six geese came out of the water and moved in his direction as well.

Lots of traffic today!

Ian got back on the path and out of their way, but the geese stopped and stared at him. Maybe they felt threatened and needed more space to get by. He side-stepped completely to the dirt on the other side of the path and waited. That's when the larger goose—most likely the mother—moved in Ian's direction, followed by the smaller geese.

"Are you coming to say hello?" Ian asked.

Mama Goose didn't look stable and Ian didn't want to be pecked to death, so he turned and walked in the opposite direction on the trail. He glanced behind him and noticed the geese were still trailing him so he picked up the pace.

A minute later a woman with a poodle approached.

Ian smiled. "Good morning."

"Good morning," she said.

The poodle suddenly pulled in Ian's direction, yanking the woman in the process. The dog knocked Ian into a tree, but fortunately he was able to grab onto a tree branch to keep himself from falling over.

"Fluffy!" she said, trying to restrain her dog but failing horribly.

The dog licked Ian's left leg a few times and then jumped over to his right leg for a little more licking. Ian reached down and scratched Fluffy on the head. "She's friendly."

"I'm *so* sorry! She's never done that before."

"No problem," said Ian. "Looks like I have a new friend."

"Did you bathe in peanut butter or something?"

Ian chuckled. "Not today."

The woman said goodbye and dragged Fluffy away.

Odd.

Ian was certain it couldn't have been his scent. The only thing different about him was—

No way.

Could it have been Billy's experimental cologne? Was that why Mama Goose was looking at him that way?

Ian's phone rang and he eyed the caller ID.

"Hi, Dad."

"Son, we're in Florence at the moment and guess who your mother and I are with?"

He could hear his dad's voice bouncing off the walls and the sound of people around him speaking in Italian. He had no clue who they were with.

"The Pope?"

"Ha! Good one, son. No, not the Pope. We're with David."

Who the heck was David?

Ian started wracking his brain trying to think of all of the Davids his family knew. But that was just it; he didn't know *any* at all. Must be someone famous.

David Beckham? David Bowie? David Hasselhoff? David Letterman?

"Son, are you there?"

"Yeah," answered Ian. "Which David are you talking about?"

"Which David? *The* David. Michelangelo's David. David!"

"Oh…the statue."

His parents were in the Accademia Gallery in Florence. He should have known. If his dad started lecturing him on sculpting or pottery he was going to hang up.

"You *know* it's not just any statue—it's a masterpiece. *This* is what I'm talking about, son. This is the level of work you need to do if you want to be somebody."

Ian couldn't believe his father was suggesting that if he wasn't as good as Michelangelo he was a nobody. He was speechless.

"That's why you made the right decision of becoming a teacher," his dad continued. "Get those crazy gallery ideas out of your head. Teaching is safe and the safe route is the smart route. Anything else is foolish."

"Foolish."

"Yeah, foolish. Gotta go."

His dad disconnected and Ian stared at the phone.

Unbelievable.

What happened to parents who told their kids they could be whatever they wanted to be when they grew up? Ian had converted the bedroom into a workshop but, truth be told, he felt like an amateur working in that space. He preferred—and needed—a larger workspace. He longed to have his own gallery too, but hadn't been able to muster up the courage to go for it. One thing stopped Ian: the discouraging words of his father that echoed in his head.

Teaching is safe and the safe route is the smart route. Anything else is foolish.

Ian cut his walk short, now more motivated than ever to continue work on the lighthouse. But first things first. He entered his house and scrubbed his body in the shower.

*****

The next evening Sara waited in the lobby of Buca di Beppo, an American restaurant chain specializing in Italian-American food and family-style portions. She had received a text from Bert that he was running fifteen minutes late. She relaxed in a chair by the front door and admired the fun vintage photographs on the wall. Her eyes traveled around the area and stopped on the white sculpture sitting on the counter in front of the hostess—the head of some famous Italian, she would guess.

Uh oh.

Sara's mind drifted to sculptors and then her new neighbor, Ian. She shouldn't be thinking about him before a date. Or at all. She had made up her mind about how far that relationship was going to go.

Nowhere.

Her phone rang and she pulled it out of her purse. Maybe Bert was running later than he originally thought. No. It was her co-worker, Becky.

"Hi Becky," she answered.

"Hey," said Becky. "You have a minute?"

"Yeah. I'm meeting someone for dinner and he's running late. And no, it's not Ian."

Becky laughed. "Very funny. I know it's not Ian."

"Oh?" Sara paused for a moment, thinking about what Becky said. "How do you know that?"

"I figured as much, since you told me you were just neighbors. Speaking of which, I hung out with him for a little while last night after you left."

"Yeah?"

"Okay, we shut the place down."

Sara felt some jealousy making its way into her system. No need to be jealous.

You're the one who chose to be friends. It's the best thing to do, so get over it!

"Are you there?" asked Becky.

"Yes. I'm here."

"Good. I was wondering…if you wouldn't mind my going out with him."

"Go out with him?"

"Did you change your mind about being friends?" asked Becky. "Because if you did, I—"

"No!" she said, a little too excitedly. "He's a friend—nothing more. Go for it!"

She felt like a cheerleader now. Where were the freaking pom-poms?

"Really?" asked Becky, obviously surprised by the answer.

"Absolutely! I have no interest in going out with him."

She could hear Becky blow out a deep breath. "Great! I felt funny calling and asking you, but I wouldn't go out with him without checking with you first. Thanks! Okay, I'll let you go. Enjoy your date!"

"Do you want his phone number?

"I already have it. He gave me his card last night."

"Oh…okay." She smiled at Bert who entered the restaurant. "The person I'm meeting is here—I need to get going."

They said their goodbyes and disconnected. Sara couldn't help but wonder if she was making a mistake by not giving Ian a chance. The doubts began to creep back into her head. But really, Becky going out with Ian would be a blessing in disguise. That would prevent her from becoming more than friends with her new neighbor, which was what she wanted. Wasn't it?

I'm a mess.

Never mind that. She needed to focus on Bert now. He was thirty years old and a celebrity personal trainer. He also explained in his email chats with Sara that he had worked out with some of the big CEOs of Silicon Valley as well a few players from the San Jose Sharks hockey team and the San Jose Earthquakes soccer team. She wondered how a guy like that could have self-control inside of a restaurant where the food smelled so amazing.

I guess I'm going to find out!

Bert walked toward Sara, smiling. She eyed his clothes.

Oh God.

He was wearing sweats.

Yes, they were fancy designer sweats—some would call it a warm-up suit—but still! This was a date. She wasn't that picky. She would have been perfectly fine with jeans and a designer t-shirt! Like the way Ian looked the other night.

Get your mind off Ian!

"Hi, Sara," he said. He pointed to his sweats. "Sorry about the way I'm dressed."

Good boy. That's what I want to hear.

"My training session went a half hour over," he added. "I didn't have time to go home and change."

"No worries."

Bert analyzed Sara's body. "You're shorter than I thought."

Someone just lost their points. Where the hell did that come from?

"You mentioned you were five-seven in your profile."

She looked down at her body. "I am."

Bert stared at Sara. It made her nervous.

"In certain shoes," she added.

"Uh huh," he said, checking her out from head to toe again.

The hostess approached and smiled. "Ready, Bert?"

"Yes," he said. "Thank you, Dina."

They were on a first name basis? Something was odd here.

Sara and Bert followed the hostess into the kitchen and Sara stopped.

Bert turned back and waved her through. "Come on!

They have a special booth for us here."

Sara looked around. "In the kitchen?"

Bert laughed. "Trust me, you'll love it."

Sara followed Bert and "Dina" and they sat in a booth directly across from the cooking area *in* the kitchen. It was odd at first, but it only took a few minutes to realize how unique and exciting it was.

After the hostess walked away Sara turned to Bert. "Lots of action in here."

Bert smiled proudly. "This is where all of the magic takes place. Smells amazing, doesn't it?"

That was an understatement. Sara wanted to eat everything she saw pass by on a plate.

A man who appeared to be the chef walked over and shook Bert's hand. "A pleasure to see you again, Bert."

"You too."

The chef smiled at Sara. "Who do you have with you today?"

"I'm Sara," she said, extending her hand and wondering why he said "today" at the end of the sentence. Did Bert come here every day? Did he bring all of his dates to Buca di Beppo? Was he one of the owners?

What's his last name again? Hmmm—I can't remember. Bert Buca? Or Bert Di Beppo? What the heck did Buca di Beppo mean anyway? Is his real name Buca but people call him Bert?

It was definitely possible. Sara thought of her Chinese hair stylist. Her real name was Chin but she preferred to be called Lisa.

"A pleasure to meet you," said the chef. "You're in for a special treat and I'll be right back with something for your enjoyment."

"Sounds great," said Sara.

Bert adjusted his seating position and winced.

"You okay?" asked Sara.

He looked like he was in a lot of pain.

Bert nodded. "I had surgery and I'm a little uncomfortable in…" He adjusted his body again and groaned. "…Certain…" He adjusted himself again and grunted. "…positions. I'll be okay. Mind over matter…"

The guy just had surgery and he's out on a date? What kind of surgery? And why didn't he cancel the date? He looked like he was suffering big time.

"If you're in a lot of pain we can do this another time. Your health is more important."

"I'll be fine. The drugs will kick in soon. But for the moment my ass is on fire."

Huh?

Sara tilted her head and stared down toward his butt in the booth, trying to figure out what the heck kind of surgery he had.

"It's not easy being this good-looking," he continued.

Did he really say that?

"It takes hard work, discipline, and a lot of money to look this good. In my case, forty grand."

"Forty—"

"For an ass implant."

Sara laughed. "Very funny."

"Seriously."

Sara couldn't help but look down at the new ass he was sitting on but really couldn't see anything at all! "Seriously?"

"Oh yeah," he answered proudly.

"An ass implant? As in like…replacing your ass…with a new ass?"

"That's right. Everybody's doing them, men and women."

Who is everybody? Before today, I didn't know anyone doing it. And why would someone get an ass implant?

"It's going to be amazing once the swelling goes down and the scars and temporary deformities fade away. I'll have to hit the tanning booth a few times before I slip on my Speedo and head to the beach."

"Speedo?"

"Lime green."

Sara didn't even want to picture that. It took all the effort she possessed not to shiver in revulsion and laugh at the absurdity.

She scratched the side of her face and stared at him. "I don't get it. You're a well known personal trainer. You certainly should be able to get your…*butt*…the way you want it, without having to resort to surgery."

Bert shook his head. "No way. There are certain features

of my new ass that couldn't possibly be obtained by even the most complex and highly-structured squat and lunge exercises. Believe me, I would know. Genes are genes. Do you know how many muscles are in the ass?"

"Uh—no."

"A lot. And there's no one exercise that works them all. Why try to kill myself when there's an easy solution? Plus, I'll be able to get more business too with my new ass. All I need to do is flex it and people will be signing up for my personal training left and right."

Her mind was screaming *fraud!*

"Do you need business that bad?" she asked. "I thought you were a celebrity trainer and people were lining up to hire you?"

"Ten years ago, yes. Even five years ago. But now that I'm forty, it is really difficult to—"

"Forty? Your profile said you were thirty."

This date was going downhill and fast and they hadn't even started the appetizers yet. This guy was ridiculous. Sara could handle some imperfections—everybody had flaws. But dishonesty? And something so superficial as an ass implant?

No way.

"People are so hung up on age," said Bert. "Am I right or am I right?"

Bert laughed at himself and then winced. "Ouch."

"Well…"

"I know for a fact that most women do *not* like the

number forty. You probably put the maximum age of the person you were seeking at thirty-nine. Am I right or am I right?"

Yes. He was right and he was right. But she sure as hell wasn't going to tell him that.

"But you could have put thirty-five or something much closer to your actual age."

"Nah. Why? This gives me more options with the younger ones." He winked.

Sara analyzed Bert for a few moments. "Do you have any other fake body parts?"

"My calves."

Sara tried to look under the table but couldn't see a thing.

Damn table!

Bert nodded. "One of the hardest parts to build on a man…the calves. Ever notice how some of the huge body builders have giant chests and arms but no calves? Now I don't have to worry about it. Oh, I forgot…I also had otoplasty."

This guy was a winner. Sara gave him the I-have-no-idea-what-the-hell-that-is look.

Bert grabbed one of his ear lobes. "Ear surgery. They were sticking out too much. When I was younger the kids called me Big Ear Bert. Not anymore!"

He forgot he had ear surgery? How do you *forget* you had ear surgery? They needed to stop talking before Sara completely lost her appetite. Thank God the chef returned with the first course—the topic needed to be changed. Sara was certain this was going nowhere. She would enjoy the dinner and that would be it with Bert.

"Please enjoy the crostini with fontina and orange marmalade."

Sara laughed and thought of Ian and his Aunt Marmaduke.

The chef raised an eyebrow.

"Sorry," she said. "I heard marmalade and I thought of Marmaduke."

"I don't understand," said the chef. "The cartoon dog?"

"Yes, sorry. Inside joke."

Sara felt bad. The chef was so sweet and the food looked amazing and she hoped he didn't take it the wrong way. She analyzed her thoughts and tried to figure out why her brain went back to Ian again.

Hmmm.

Time to distract the chef from the awkwardness.

Sara pointed to the platter on the table. "This looks amazing. Thank you so much."

The chef smiled. "My pleasure. Enjoy."

Mission accomplished.

Sara enjoyed the food, but the company—not so much. Forty-five minutes later she bid Bert and his brand new ass farewell forever and walked home. She walked down Campbell Avenue and stopped in Orchard Valley Coffee to grab a cup of tea. One step into the place and she saw Ian.

He was sitting with a beautiful young woman, looking like they were having the time of their lives.

She felt jealousy creep through her body and wondered who the woman was. Maybe she should call her a girl—she barely looked eighteen.

Oh God. The woman-girl-thing flipped her hair back. That move was so old it had cobwebs on it. He couldn't possibly fall for it.

Ian's smile widened.

Great. The sucker fell for it.

Sara realized she was standing in the doorway staring at them. Before she could move or hide the door opened behind her and a group of four people came in, pushing her farther inside. She couldn't escape now. Especially since Ian looked in her direction.

He did a double-take and stood, now moving toward Sara.

Look natural. Appear happy. Not shocked.

"Hi, Sara," he said, looking a little surprised. "Great to see you."

"You too," she said.

She looked back behind him. She sure misjudged the guy. She remembered what he had told her. *Dating's tough.* Didn't look that difficult from this vantage point.

"You come here often?" she asked.

God. That sounded like a pickup line. What were you thinking?

"It's one of my favorite places," he answered. "I'm here a few times a week."

I bet you are.

It looked like he was having a difficult time with that jiggly girl. And now Becky was going to call and ask him out? Maybe she should warn Becky.

"Sara?"

Oh no. Ian said something and I missed it.

"Sorry," she said. "You said something?"

"Yeah. You left in a hurry last night."

"Oh, that. Right. I had to go back to the house to let Kili out for a pee."

He raised a suspicious eyebrow.

"What?" she asked.

"I remember you telling me she peed before you got to the festival. Remember? Then she was on her hind legs at my door barking for me."

"Huh? Oh, right. Well, with big dogs come *big* bladders. Better to err on the side of caution or you might end up with a flooded house!"

She laughed and slapped Ian on the arm.

Okay, that was the most pathetic lie ever.

Ian nodded, not looking convinced. "I should get back but I wanted to say hi."

"Okay."

Ian turned to head back to join the floozy-woman-girl-thing.

Sara changed her mind about the cup of tea and headed out. A gallon of ice cream sounded much better. Besides, it would be too distracting with Ian there. She peeked back through the window on the sidewalk before she crossed the street and watched as Ian's "companion" did another hair flip.

Amazing.

This guy had no problem getting dates. Why couldn't she find a date for her wedding? Was it really that difficult? She was a good person and had a lot of positive qualities. And to think she'd considered Ian as a possible date for the wedding after his heroic effort on her front porch. No way. He'd lost her respect. She wondered what she would say the next time she saw him.

"Stop it," she said to herself, startling an older man walking by. She forced a smile at the man. "Not you."

No more thinking of the neighbor!

That was easier said than done.

Chapter Seven

The next morning Ian sat at his kitchen table, his arm extended horizontally across the top of it like he was getting ready for someone to extract blood.

Pacing back and forth, Billy scratched his chin and mumbled something.

"Can we get this over with?" asked Ian. "I'm hungry."

"I'm gathering my thoughts before I proceed."

"Gather this! That cologne you concocted has some serious problems. Women don't even pay attention to me but household pets and barnyard animals want to get freaky with me."

"Don't exaggerate."

"I'm not exaggerating and I couldn't take it anymore, so I scrubbed it off my body.

Billy shook his head. "You can scrub all you want but that won't do a thing. Your body absorbed the cologne and there are special components that allow it to stay in your system for over thirty days."

Ian blinked. "Can you invent something to help me kill you in your sleep?"

Billy chuckled. "Quiet now. I need to focus."

Ian let out a deep breath and waited for Billy to test his new product. Billy had somehow convinced him—with a phone call this morning at seven—to be the rat for his next experiment. More like bribery, since he promised he would bring over his favorite bagels.

"And I don't get it," said Ian. "You were looking for a way to stimulate hair growth. Now you want to get rid of hair. Make up your mind."

Billy tapped his temple with his index finger. "I've got a thousand ideas in here waiting to happen, so listen up. This is permanent hair removal with a simple liquid application. Ten times faster than laser. A thousand times cheaper. With no pain or side effects."

Right.

Ian knew Billy was a smart guy but this sounded too good to be true. And why couldn't he go test it on women since they were the typical customers for such a product? Women usually had a higher tolerance for pain too, in case something went wrong. Billy didn't answer that question and offered fresh bagels. Ian was a sucker for bagels. Cinnamon raisin. Blueberry. Asiago cheese. It didn't matter. He didn't have the willpower to say no. Ever.

Ian eyed the bag of bagels on the other end of the table and inhaled through his nose. "Why don't we eat while you think about it? Take your time." Ian stretched to try to grab the bag of bagels. "No rush."

Billy jumped and slid the bag away further. "This will

only take a minute." He paced a little more and then stopped. "Okay, got it." He grabbed a small spray bottle from the crate he brought in with him and moved closer to Ian's arm. "Oops, almost forgot." He turned back to the crate and took out a bag of cotton balls and a bottle of alcohol. He applied the alcohol to a cotton ball and wiped Ian's arm with it. "There."

Ian eyed the spot and then his eyes shot up at Billy. "You sure this isn't going to hurt?"

"Yes, I'm sure. Although I make no guarantees."

"What?"

Before Ian could object Billy sprayed the small area of his arm with the hair-removal liquid.

Ian screamed. "Oh my God! That burns like a son of a —"

"Okay, okay. Not good."

"Definitely not good! My arm feels like it's on fire!"

Bang! Bang! Bang!

Billy's head jerked toward the wall. "What the hell was that?"

"My crabby neighbor. But forget about her, this stuff is eating me alive!"

Billy paced back and forth. "I told you not to exaggerate. I didn't consider the possibility of the chemicals having a bad reaction when they mixed with the alcohol from the cotton ball. Interesting…"

"Interesting? That's all you have to say?" Ian jumped up.

"I need to rinse this off. My arm is burning."

"No! For the love of science!"

"Yes! For the love of God!"

Ian placed his arm under the faucet and turned the water on. His scream this time was louder than the first one. "Ahhhhhhh! Shit! What's going on here?"

"I was going to tell you! I was unaware of the reaction when mixed with alcohol but I knew, based on past experimentation, what would happen when water came into the equation."

"Help me, this is burning like hell."

"Do you have ranch dressing?"

"Do I look like a freaking salad to you?"

"I'm serious. Do you want me to help you or not?"

"Yes! Fridge!"

Billy got the ranch dressing from the refrigerator, popped the top, and squirted a liberal amount over the affected area."

Ian sighed, then smiled. "Thank you. Thank you. Yes. That did the trick."

There was a loud knock at the door.

Ian held his arm out in front of him horizontally so the ranch dressing didn't drip off and walked over, opening the front door.

Sara stood there with her hands on her hips. "How many times are you going to wake me up this summer? I—" Her eyes dropped to his arm with the ranch dressing.

Ian followed her eyes and opened his mouth to speak.

She held up her hand to stop him. "I don't even wanna know. Really. Keep the noise down or I'll report you to the homeowners association."

Billy snuck up behind Ian, still holding the bottle of ranch dressing in his hand. He had a little bit of ranch on his finger, so he licked it. His eyes lit up. "A female! Please come in! Do you have any unwanted hair?"

Sara squished her eyebrows together. "Keep your kinky stuff behind closed doors and we won't have any problems."

"It's not what you think," said Ian.

"Right." Sara stormed off.

Ian closed the door and sighed. "Why the heck did you ask her if she had unwanted hair?"

"You told me it may be better to test it on females and I agree with you now. It was a harmless question."

"But as a conversation starter? It sounds *really* bad—perverted even. Ever thought of introducing yourself first? She must think you're a freak."

"Right!" Billy pointed at Ian's arm. "You opened the door with ranch dressing on your arm. Who's the freak here, mister?"

Billy was right. Ian must be the freak in Sara's eyes.

He liked Sara and was concerned about her—she didn't look happy. In fact, she looked more than angry. It wasn't his intention to wake her up but it almost seemed as if there was something else on her mind. Hopefully he would be able to fix it the next time he saw her. She seemed a little off when he saw her at Orchard Valley Coffee last night. She wasn't herself and looked like she was hiding something. She seemed distant. The kiss with her was amazing and he was certain she felt the same way. Especially since she was the one who initiated it.

"Okay, let's forget about it and eat,' said Ian. "I need to work on the lighthouse today."

After they finished off their coffee and the bagels Billy left and Ian's phone rang. It wasn't anyone in his contacts but he decided to answer it anyway.

"Hello?"

"Hi Ian, this is Becky."

"Oh. Hi." Ian was surprised to hear from her. They had ended up walking around the art & wine festival and chatting after Sara had left. She was kind, but to be honest, she was a little bit odd. Nothing like Sara, that was for sure.

"What a nice surprise to hear from you," he lied.

Becky laughed. "I enjoyed hanging out with you. Hopefully I didn't talk your ear off."

You did. "No, no, no."

She sounded relieved. "Oh, good. I tend to talk a little—or a lot—when I have a wine glass in my hand."

She snorted.

Sara's snorts were so much cuter. Becky sounded like a groundhog.

"Anyway," continued Becky. "I wanted to see if you'd like

to get together this weekend. There's an art exhibition at the Santa Clara County Fairgrounds. I thought it would be fun to go with someone who knows so much about art. You could teach me some things. Oh, and Sara said it was okay."

"What do you mean?"

"You know—I asked her if she wouldn't mind if I went out with you. I wanted to make sure after seeing you dance together but she assured me you were only friends and that I should go for it."

"Is that right?"

"Yes! Sara said she had no interest in going out with you. So, here I am calling."

No wonder Sara took off like that from the festival. No wonder she was cold with him when he saw her at the coffee place. But why? It didn't make sense. He felt something and he was positive she did too. Nothing against Becky—she was a kind person. But he had no interest in going out with her. Still, he was planning on going to the exhibition this weekend. That would be awkward if he said no to her invitation and then ran into her there. He would be okay going with her. But as friends, of course. The thought of that brought Becky's words back into his head.

Sara said she had no interest in going out with you.

"What do you say?" asked Becky. "You wanna go?"

"Why not?"

Ian used the next few hours to work on the sculpture and he was finally making some great progress. He smiled, thinking of his grandparents, Carl and Louise. They were two of his favorite people, sweet, kind, generous, and an inspiration, having been married fifty years. He was so looking forward to their anniversary party next week. Especially the part where he surprised them with the sculpture of the lighthouse where Carl proposed to Louise.

"Woof!"

Ian smiled again at the sound of Kili and his mind was back on Sara again. He wondered what she was doing at the moment. He needed to find out what was going on with her. She told Becky she didn't want to go out with him. But she was fooling herself if she thought he was going to give up that easily.

Chapter Eight

Sara couldn't remember the last time she went out on a lunch date. To her, going out in the evening felt more romantic. But this felt safer considering how the date with Buster went.

John seemed to have *plenty* of potential. He'd been a consultant for the last ten years, owned his own business and his own home, and ran ten miles a day. She made sure he didn't live with his mother before she agreed to meet him at Outback Steakhouse.

She entered the front door and spotted John waiting for her off to the right. He obviously recognized her, moving in her direction.

"Hi, Sara," he said, smiling and waving with his free hand. His other hand was holding a briefcase. Odd. Did he come straight from work? It looked like it. He looked business casual—wearing black dress slacks and a matching black polo shirt with his company logo on the right side of the chest. He was self-employed so maybe he came from a client meeting. But why didn't he stick the briefcase in his trunk? Hopefully he wasn't going to try to sell her something.

She squashed the thought and leaned in to hug him.

"Hi, John. Nice to meet you in person."

John jumped back, avoiding her hug. "Yes!" He nervously pointed toward the reception area. "They have a table ready for us."

That was weird. "Okay."

Was John not a hugging type of person? That would certainly be a deal breaker. Sara was affectionate. Maybe he was a little shy on the first date. She tried not to read into it too much. The guy was attractive and his straight dark hair was slicked back. He had sort of a sexy Andy Garcia vibe going on.

They followed the hostess and she pointed to their table. "Here you go."

Sara sat and the hostess handed her a menu. "Thanks."

John remained standing and waved off the menu when the hostess turned to him. "I don't need one, thanks."

The hostess smiled and nodded. "I never look at the menu either. I always have the same thing too!"

"It's not that." He pointed to the menu and crinkled his nose. "That thing is dirtier than a toilet seat."

The hostess stared at him, probably wondering if he was serious. Sara was staring too.

John had mentioned in his online profile that he had a sense of humor. Was he trying to be funny? This wasn't funny. It was embarrassing.

The hostess now looked confused, staring at the menu. She flipped it over to the other side. "Looks okay to me."

"I have a handheld microscope in the car. You want me to go get it?"

The hostess held up her hand. "That's quite all right. Enjoy your meal." She rolled her eyes and walked away.

John pulled a napkin from his front pocket, unfolded it, and placed it over the surface of his chair. After he sat on top of the napkin, he pulled out another napkin from his pocket and placed it on the chair to his right before setting his briefcase on top of it. Then he proceeded to inspect the things on the table. He pulled out a third napkin from his pocket and carefully pushed his silverware to the end of the table.

This guy carries a lot of napkins.

"I can tell you what's on the menu if you want," said Sara, pretending not to notice his odd behavior.

"No need," said John. "I saw it online last night and memorized it."

Sara stared down at the extensive menu with the countless items and descriptions and raised her gaze back up to John. "Memorized it? You mean like…every single item?"

He nodded. "Easy peasy. The menus for The Cheesecake Factory and Red Robin were a little more difficult."

"You do it for every restaurant?"

"I haven't touched a menu in ten years. I also haven't been sick in ten years. Connection? You bet."

"Huh.' She analyzed the guy for a moment. "You even

memorize how it's prepared and what it comes with?"

John nodded.

"Really…" She stared down at the menu again, scanning some of the items. "So if I ask you how the baby back ribs are prepared you'd be able to tell me?"

He didn't even hesitate. "The chefs rub them down with their signature blend of seventeen secret spices and then smoke them until they are tender and bursting with flavor."

Sara's mouth was hanging open.

"Then they brush them with their Outback homemade tangy barbecue sauce," he continued.

"I—"

"It comes with Aussie fries."

This guy was amazing. And he did this so he wouldn't have to touch the menu. But something was puzzling her.

"How come you don't figure out what you want to eat and then remember the one single item?" she asked. "That's so much easier."

"What if they run out of that item? Plus, I like to have the option of changing my mind. I could get here and be in the mood for something completely different from what I was thinking last night. Especially after seeing or smelling the food."

The waitress arrived and they placed their drink and food orders. Coincidentally, John ordered the baby back ribs while Sara opted for a burger and fries.

Sara watched as John prepared the eating area. He

clicked open his briefcase and pulled out a small bottle, spraying the part of the table in front of him. He wiped it clean and then pulled out his own placemat, setting it neatly in front of him. Next came his own utensils and salt and pepper shakers. Last came his own bottle of ketchup.

"There," he said. "Perfect."

A man at the table next to them sneezed.

Sara swung around. "Bless you."

When she turned back around, John had a blue surgeon's mask securely fastened around his nose and mouth.

She jumped. "You scared the crap out of me."

"Sorry—just protecting myself. Unfortunately, you have been contaminated."

Sara studied John for a moment. "Don't you think this is a little overkill?"

He shook his head. "Sneezes travel eighty miles per hour. His germs have already entered your body and are traveling around inside of you, looking for a place to set up camp. Soon they will be roasting marshmallows, along with your immune system. You'll be sick within three days."

"And what if it was a sneeze caused by allergies or dust?"

He nodded and almost looked to be appreciating her question. "I'm not willing to take that chance."

Sara was all for protecting herself and trying to stay healthy but this was ridiculous. What a way to live. This wasn't living at all!

"I can see this bothers you," he said.

"I wouldn't say it bothers me. I just can't see myself living the way you're living."

He nodded again. "I see. I guess what you're trying to say is that we have no future together."

He was just figuring this out now? Sara had suspicions the moment he avoided her hug when she arrived!

"I would never try to impose this on you," he continued. "But you'll have to live with the fact that you're not as healthy as me."

I can live with that.

She wondered what his home was like. Most likely as sterile as a hospital.

"What about the people who bring germs into your house?" she asked. "When your friends visit?"

"I rarely have guests over."

Not a surprise.

"But when I do," he continued. "They have to take off their shoes before they come in, since that's how many germs travel inside. Once they leave I clean all of the surfaces and objects they touched inside the house."

"You memorize that too?"

"Always. The only thing I'm not sure of is what they touched in the guest bathroom so I scrub everything from floor to ceiling. It takes about two hours but it helps me sleep at night."

"So I must assume that you don't have any pets, right?"

"Pets! No contaminating hairy beasts in my house, ever!

That is something I will never understand, how people can stand cats and dogs for the sake of not being alone. No way."

He looked repulsed. Poor guy, paranoid of everything.

The guy was right—they had absolutely no future together. She could tell him he shouldn't live his life in fear but she was doing the same thing when it came to Ian.

Oh God. I'm living my life in fear.

She liked Ian. A lot. But she feared it wouldn't work out and then she'd have to move again. Why should she judge Germaphobe John for the way he was living? She couldn't.

They ate their meals and the waitress brought the bill. John insisted on swiping his own credit card since he didn't want anyone else touching it. He never carried cash. It had just as many germs as a vending machine.

As they said their hug-less goodbyes in the parking lot, there was something that Sara wanted to know. She couldn't believe she was going to ask it. "I'm curious. Do you avoid kissing people because of the germs in the mouth?"

He stared at her for a moment. "Are you saying you want to kiss me goodbye?"

"No! I mean…no. Just curious what you did with your last girlfriend. I mean, if you've had one. Ever."

He nodded. "Yes, I *did* have a girlfriend, thank you very much. Her name was Mona and we had an amazing three week love affair. We also had an agreement that we would both shower thoroughly and gargle with antiseptic before we became…intimate."

"That certainly doesn't leave room for spontaneity. You never had the urge to grab Mona and kiss her as you strolled hand in hand on the beach?"

"We never went to the beach. People pee in the ocean and I don't want to be anywhere near that."

"Of course."

Sara loved spontaneity. She walked to her car and thought of the kiss she shared with Ian. The kiss *she* initiated. She certainly didn't plan that ahead of time. Maybe that's why it was so exhilarating. Heck, it was more than exhilarating. It was hot. She wouldn't mind having another one of those kisses but it wasn't going to happen.

Ian was off limits. And hopefully she wouldn't run into him when she got home.

Chapter Nine

Sara had a good feeling about her date this evening. Out of all of the men so far Daniel was the only one who asked about her goals in life and her dreams during their email exchange. Of course, she wasn't going to tell him that her only goal at the moment was to find a date for Tiffany's wedding. But still, it felt as though he really wanted to get to know her, which was refreshing and made her look forward to the date even more.

Daniel offered to pick Sara up at her home but she took Ian's advice and met him at Thai Orchid, one of her favorite places in Campbell, across from Outback Steakhouse.

How cool that my new home is close to so many amazing restaurants! Does Ian like Thai food? What is he doing right now? Where the hell did those thoughts come from?

Daniel walked in and headed in her direction. Her gaze dropped down to his swinging hand carrying a small box and some flowers. She wondered if the flowers were expensive.

The thought of Buster—Mr. Money Bags—made her laugh. What a loser.

"Did I do something funny?" asked Daniel.

"No, no," said Sara, trying to clear the smile from her

face. She held out her hand, in case Daniel didn't like hugs. "Nice to meet you."

He grabbed her hand and kissed it. "Nice to meet you too." He handed her flowers and a small box of chocolates. "These are for you."

"Thank you, that's sweet of you."

She'd received flowers plenty of times in the past, but no man had ever given her chocolate on the first date.

A man after my own heart.

The hostess approached and took them past the large money tree and the statue of Buddha to their table.

Daniel pointed to the private room behind the silky green curtains. "Do you mind if we sit in one of the booths in the back room?"

"That's fine," said the waitress. "Follow me."

Sara was okay with it too. There was more privacy and it would be easier to talk. Maybe he was a romantic.

After they ordered dinner and tea, Sara picked up the flowers and smelled them. "Thanks again for the flowers. They're beautiful." She smelled them again and smiled.

"My pleasure. I made the bouquet myself."

Sara stared at the flowers—a mix of gardenias, pink tulips, and green poms. He even wrapped them in raffia. Then she studied Daniel.

"I know what you're thinking," said Daniel. "So before you come to the conclusion that I'm gay, let me explain."

Wow. He was good. "Okay."

"My grandmother was a florist for over forty years," he explained. "When I was young I spent a lot of time at her shop. In fact, the first job I ever had was working as her assistant. I learned a lot about flowers—how to care for them, cut them, arrange them. And I learned something even more amazing...flowers have an impact on emotional health."

"That doesn't surprise me. I don't think there was ever a time when I didn't smile after receiving flowers. See." She pointed to her smiling mouth.

Daniel laughed. "Exactly! And those smiles and those thoughts release certain positive chemicals in the brain. This is something that's universal. It's difficult to find someone who doesn't like flowers."

"I agree."

The waitress returned with their appetizer egg rolls and they both helped themselves to one.

Sara took a bite of her egg roll and admired the man in front of her. He wore Dockers and a tan polo shirt that matched his brown eyes. His hair was short and straight—also matching his eyes—and she could see a touch of gray hair coming in around the temples. It was refreshing to see a guy who didn't try to cover up those gray hairs with some color. She had to admit that the date was off to a great start. There were no red flags and Daniel seemed like a kind and sensitive person so far. A thousand times better than Asshat Calvin, Buster Money Bags, and New-Butt Bert.

The thought of those three dates made her laugh.

"I'm going to get a complex if you keep doing that," said Daniel.

"What?"

"Laughing for no reason."

"Sorry," said Sara. "I've been on a few dates lately that were pathetic and I had another flashback."

"Oh…"

Sara smiled. "I'm really enjoying myself so far."

Daniel matched her smile. "Me too. I had a good feeling when I stumbled upon your profile. Geography teachers can't be all that bad."

"You're a wise man." She smiled and raised her tea cup to his. They toasted and started their main course.

"Are you enjoying your summer vacation so far?" asked Daniel, scraping some Pad Thai onto his plate.

"Very much. Teachers work hard during the school year—even on evenings after school and on weekends—so this is our time to disconnect. We need this time badly to avoid burnout."

Daniel nodded. "Teachers should be paid more. I think they have one of the most important jobs. And it can't be easy dealing with teenagers and their cell phones."

Sara raised her tea cup to his again. "Thank you! I love your empathy." She could see Daniel was studying her. "What?"

"I was thinking about the summer and, well, I have a

vacation house in Lake Tahoe. We should go sometime."

Sara blinked.

"Sorry," continued Daniel. "That came out of nowhere."

"It's okay."

"Call me crazy, since I just met you but I like you and I feel comfortable with you. But here I am already inviting you to go away with me."

"It's fine. The truth is I'm enjoying your company too. But let's not rush things. Let's get through dinner and see where we go from there."

"Good plan."

Sara was caught off guard by the invite but she had to admit that a weekend—or a week!—in Lake Tahoe sounded amazing. And Daniel seemed like a good guy. Not as fun as Ian and a little older, but…

Crap. Get your mind off Ian, woman! You're on a date.

Yes, Ian was hotter than Daniel and she had a lot more in common with Ian but Daniel was a good man. And responsible, obviously, since he had two homes! Not that she was a gold-digger or anything. She smiled, thinking of Calvin's mother.

Daniel pointed to Sara's face. "You're doing it again."

Sara winced. "Sorry. I'm beginning to realize I spend *way* too much time in my head."

They finished a lovely dinner and Daniel suggested they go for a walk through downtown Campbell. They walked by

Recycle Bookstore and stopped at the stop sign. A woman walked by with a Golden Retriever. Sara smiled and thought of Kili, who was most likely at home snoring up a storm in her big doggy bed.

"Beautiful dog," said Daniel.

"Do you have one?" asked Sara.

"Had."

"Oh. Sorry."

"That's okay. She was fifteen when she died and she lived a good life."

He liked dogs. Good. Ian liked dogs.

Stop it!

Daniel pointed to Orchard Valley Coffee. "Care for a cup of coffee or tea to wrap up the evening?"

Sara stared at the windows of the place. Too bad she couldn't see through them. Ian loved that place and it would be awkward if he were there. Should she take a chance?

But why should it be awkward? They were just neighbors. Nothing else. It's not as if she *liked* the guy! Okay, she liked him a little. And it wouldn't be such a bad thing if he was there anyway. In fact, it would be a sign if he was in there.

Yeah. It would mean that they lived two blocks from the place. That's not serendipity! That's logic! It wouldn't be a coincidence at all.

"Sara?"

"Huh?"

"Are you up in your head again?"

Sara nodded. "Guilty." She smiled and pointed to the coffee place. "A cup of tea sounds great."

They crossed the street and headed inside. Standing in line, Sara looked around the place, pretending to be admiring the interior and ambiance.

Ian wasn't there.

She let out a deep breath and turned around. She stared into the back of a man whose hair seemed familiar. It was standing up in a hundred directions. Sexy hair, just like—

The man turned around and flashed that sexy grin.

"What did I tell you?" asked Ian.

Sara was caught off guard. "What?"

"I told you we'd be running into each other often." Ian looked at Daniel and his state changed. His smile was gone in an instant and something odd flashed across his face.

Was that jealousy?

Ian held out his hand. "Hi. Ian McBride."

Daniel stared at his hand for a brief moment and then accepted his handshake. "Daniel…"

Odd. What was happening here?

Daniel and Ian continued to stare at each other for a few more moments but then Daniel broke the silence. "What type of tea would you like, Sara?"

It took a huge effort for Sara to get the words to come out of her mouth. "It's late so I'll have chamomile."

Ian turned his attention back to Sara. "Enjoy the evening." Ian gave Daniel the death stare and turned around to place his order with the cashier.

Okay, that was awkward.

Ian was jealous—which wasn't always a bad thing at all!

"You're smiling," said Daniel.

"Huh? Oh, it's just…I *love* chamomile. Love, love, love it."

What a crock. She hated lying but what was she going to say? That she liked that guy standing in front of them but was too scared to do anything about it?

A minute later Ian grabbed two drinks from the counter and turned, heading past Sara and avoiding contact.

Two coffees? What the heck.

Sara flipped around and watched Ian walk to his table—he was with a *different* jiggly girl!

Seriously?

This one seemed even younger. And more jiggly.

That settled it, no more fantasizing about her neighbor. He dated women half his age. She barely looked legal.

Great. Miss Jiggly did the hair-flip as well as the other one.

Those two words from Ian came back and planted themselves in Sara's head.

Dating's tough.

Right.

"Sara?" asked Daniel.

She spun back around. "Yeah?"

Daniel chuckled. "Welcome back."

"Sorry," she said. "There I go again."

Daniel handed Sara her tea and they sat at a table next to the window that overlooked Campbell Avenue.

Forget about the guy.

Besides, Sara had a kind and handsome man in front of her and she should focus on him.

For the next thirty minutes they sipped their teas and talked about traveling, food, and work. Not too exciting, but she wasn't bored at all. Truthfully, Daniel was the best of all the men she had dated so far—nothing wrong with him at all. A little reserved, but was there anything wrong with that?

"Although I could tell your mind was somewhere else this evening," said Daniel. "I like you and I'd like to see you again. I think we have a lot in common and there is potential here."

"That would be great. I'd like that too."

They said their goodbyes with a kiss on the cheek and agreed to chat soon about their next get-together. Daniel was a wonderful man and there was no reason why she shouldn't go out with him again. Plus he had some serious patience for putting up with her distracted mind.

Daniel would be the perfect date to Tiffany's wedding.

Chapter Ten

Sara wanted to scream. This didn't make any sense at all. She and Daniel had agreed last night to chat soon about getting together again. Then she received this email from him this morning:

Dear Sara,

I'm sorry but I won't be able to see you again. I have a lot going on and don't want to complicate things. I wish you the best in all you do. Take care.

Daniel

That's it? Just like that? The guy didn't even have the decency to call. And was he saying that she would be complicating his life? Unbelievable. She responded with only two words:

Good luck.

She would be lying if she said the email didn't bug the

heck out of her. Yes, she was a little distracted last night but she and Daniel still had a good time. There had to be something more he wasn't saying, but it really didn't matter now. Time to move on.

She went to Home Depot to pick up a plant and some soil. Might as well be productive and replace Ian's plant that Kili ate. She was in no mood to see Ian, so she'd have to work quickly.

Ten minutes later the job was almost complete. She added a little more soil to the planter box and then pressed it down firmly around the plant with her hand. She felt good. She was able to replace Ian's plant without seeing him. That's the last thing she wanted or needed. Satisfied with the job, she grabbed the bag of soil and stood up, turning to leave.

The creak of the door and his voice stopped her. "Nice plant."

Crap.

She was *this* close to escaping. She should have tried to plant it at three in the morning. She turned slowly and eyed her neighbor. He looked like he was ready to go out, dressed sharply in designer jeans and a button down shirt that wasn't tucked it.

Handsome. Stop it!

"Glad you like it," she answered. "I did some research and this plant is supposed to be impossible to kill and most dogs leave it alone."

"I like it. Even better that it's both Ian and Kili proof."

She wiped off her hands and winced. She lifted her finger to examine it.

"What happened?"

"I guess I got a splinter from the planter box. I can't see it, but I can feel it."

He pointed to her hand. "Let me see."

Before Sara could respond he had already grabbed her hand and was inspecting the injured finger. "Yeah, I see it—it's a tiny little sucker. Hang on, don't move a muscle."

"Okay."

Ian disappeared inside his home and returned about thirty seconds later.

He grinned and held up tweezers. "Dr. Ian at your service."

"You don't have to—"

"Hold still."

"Fine, *Dr.* Ian."

What hands. Soft. Warm.

He pressed gently with the tweezers and plucked the thorn from under her skin. Then he kissed her finger. "There. All better."

He made a funny face like he had tasted something bitter and then he wiped his mouth.

"Sorry. My hands are a little dirty."

"That's okay. Doesn't bug me at all. Look."

He grabbed her finger and kissed it again. Then he

kissed the top of her hand.

I can get used to that. Can you do it again? Then you can work your way up my arm to my neck...I mean, if you're not too busy.

She lifted her finger to analyze it and rubbed the spot where the thorn was. "Thank you."

Don't make a big deal about this. Time to make an escape. Just friends.

Sara pointed toward her place. "I'd better get going." She turned and ran right into her front door.

Ian laughed. "You okay?"

"Yeah," she said, feeling her nose. "It usually helps to open the door before I enter."

"That's what I typically do."

She was going to die from embarrassment.

"Hi Sara," said Becky, approaching the house.

Sara swung around and her eyes opened wide with surprise. "Hi Becky. I wasn't expecting you."

Becky was wearing a graceful burgundy skirt just above her knees and a white sleeveless blouse. Simple and cute.

"That's because I'm here to see Ian." She smiled at him, confirming Sara's fear. "You ready to go?"

These two don't waste any time!

"Is it that time already?" Ian checked his watch. "Oh, you're fifteen minutes early. I still need to do a few things before we take off." He turned to Sara. "We're going to the art exhibition over at the fairgrounds."

"How fun," said Sara.

"I had no idea I was so early!" said Becky.

No idea at all. Right. One day they'll invent clocks to put in cars.

"Can I come in while I wait for you?" Becky continued. "I'd love to see your place."

I bet you would.

Ian shrugged. "Okay. Come on in."

Becky walked by Sara and winked at her before entering Ian's place.

Ian stuck his head back out the door. "Thanks again for the new plant. I love it." He winked and closed the door.

What's with all of this winking? You can take that wink and shove it!

Sara didn't like her thoughts. First she got an email from Daniel saying he didn't want to see her anymore, and then she watched as her friend arrived to go out with the man who was constantly on her mind. She's the one who told Becky she had no interest in going out with Ian—she should be happy for her friend. She's the one who decided she shouldn't go out with Ian herself because they were neighbors. But the more she thought about it, the more she believed she had made the biggest mistake.

*****

Thirty minutes later Ian arrived at the Santa Clara County Fairgrounds with Becky.

"I haven't been on a date in such a long time," she said,

entering the exhibition hall with Ian.

Not good. She thought they were on a date.

"Me neither," he replied, hoping it wouldn't get awkward.

He only said yes to her to be nice and because he was planning on going anyway. Hopefully the event wouldn't be too bad. He knew some of the artists who would be there, and even his friend Billy had planned on showing up.

Becky pointed to the first display after they entered, a bird bath made out of a paella pan and bicycle parts. "That's fascinating."

"This is called experimental art and the artist is expressing himself. You'll see all types here, including fine art and street art. Some of these artists are first time exhibitors, while others are internationally acclaimed."

"So it's not for sale?"

"No." Ian spotted Billy a few booths down and pointed to him. "I want to introduce you to a friend who is here."

"Sounds great."

"Billy," said Ian, approaching an artist's depiction of the universe. The planets were made up of various sizes of tennis balls, racquetballs, and ping pong balls. All of them were painted uniquely and dangling from an old TV antennae.

Billy pointed to the display. "This artist has got some serious balls displaying something like this in public."

An excruciating sound echoed throughout the exhibition hall. Ian was sure it was a hyena mating with a peacock.

Nope. It was Becky laughing.

She looked like she was losing control of her body, her shoulders bouncing up and down like a sugar-hyped-up-kid in a bouncy castle. Even if Ian would have considered this a date, it wouldn't have worked out. Becky was sweet but not his type. It would take a very eccentric man to appreciate someone like Becky.

"Who's this dynamite woman?" asked Billy.

Bingo.

Becky blushed and extended her hand. "Becky."

"I'm Billy." He accepted her hand and his eyes zeroed in on her arms. He pulled them closer to inspect. "Your arms are unusually hairy."

No!

There went any chance of these two hooking up! The guy had no tact at all. And there was a good possibility Billy was going to get kicked in the balls.

Here it comes, Billy! Protect your privates!

"Tell me about it!" said Becky. "I tried waxing them but the hair came back twice as thick! I seriously wish I had some magic formula to get rid of it. I'm too skittish to try laser."

Okay. There *was* a chance with these two.

Billy's eyes lit up. "Funny you mention it but I've been working on a revolutionary new cream that gets rid of unwanted hair."

"Really?"

"Absolutely. I'm a teacher, but besides that and most

importantly, I'm a scientist. You're a beautiful woman who will be even more beautiful once I eliminate that arm hair with my magical cream." He pointed to her face. "And you can say goodbye to that mustache too."

She ran a finger across her upper lip and smiled. "I should have you do my whole body."

He grinned and eyed her from head to toe. "It would be my pleasure."

Becky's chest heaved back and forth.

Oh my God. She looks turned on.

The smile drifted from her face and her gaze was locked with Billy's. They were having a moment and Ian felt awkward being in the middle of it. Billy was still holding onto her hand, swinging it back and forth.

Unbelievable.

His nerdy friend was good. So much for knowing what the opposite sex liked. Hell, he thought he had something good with Sara but she wanted nothing to do with him.

"I have an idea," said Billy. "How about joining me in the food court for a tasty beverage of your choice and we can discuss it further?"

"Oh…" Becky turned to Ian. "Is that okay? I know you really wanted to spend time with me."

Oh, how I longed for it. "I don't mind at all," said Ian. "I need to walk around a little bit before I'll be ready for food… or magical creams. Have fun."

And just like that they were gone.

Ian was standing there all alone wondering what the hell happened. Yes, he had no interest in Becky but he was puzzled at how easy it was for those two to connect.

He walked around for an hour, chatting with a few artists he knew and admiring some of the amazing art. Then he got a text from Billy.

-Ian! Becky and I left and we're at my place. :) Talk to you later, buddy.

Ian chuckled. "Oh. My. God."

Maybe it was better this way. Ian needed to get back to work on the lighthouse, so this was a great excuse for him to head back home.

He smiled when he thought of Billy and Becky. What were the chances? He and Sara had a connection like that but something happened at the festival to end it. She made it clear she wasn't interested. Better to avoid her so they didn't have awkward moments.

"What a shame," he said to himself.

Twenty minutes later he was home, ready to work on the lighthouse. With a flick of a switch the potter's wheel came to life again, accompanied by that old familiar squealing sound. Time was running out and he had to quit being so picky. His grandparents wouldn't notice any of the flaws he noticed anyway. And if he was going to make an exact replica it didn't have to be perfect. The real lighthouse itself was not perfect.

He had to admit, this time around, the bottom of the tower and the stairs that led to the entry looked good. He finished the top piece and carved out the openings for the windows, which looked more like giant keyholes.

Ian smiled. "Much better. Good job." He started up the wheel again to finish the crown, which was the easiest of them all. A few minutes later it was done. He placed the crown on the drying board and dipped his hands in the bucket of water, rubbing them together until the clay came off. As he wiped his hands there was banging at the door, followed by a crazy succession of doorbell rings.

"Looks like the neighbor is going psychotic again," he said to himself.

She had obviously forgotten about their amazing kiss and was back to being crabby. Hell, who was he kidding? He enjoyed seeing her even when she was pissed off.

The knocking and ringing continued.

"Hold on, would ya?" Ian opened the door, careful not to bang the wall and make the hole any bigger. Sara stood there, out of breath. She was certainly worked up this time over the noise. What a drama queen.

"Don't tell me," he said. "I woke up Sleeping Beauty from an evening nap?"

"There's something wrong with Kili," she said, her eyes tearing up. "Please help me."

Chapter Eleven

Ian felt like a world-class jerk. Sara came to him distraught, practically crying, and he opened the door and made fun of her. He knew how much Kili meant to her and he would do anything to help. The truth was he loved the dog too.

He followed Sara through her home to her back patio. Kili was pacing back and forth but didn't look like she had much coordination.

That's weird.

Ian moved closer to the dog and pet her on the head. "Poor girl, she's trembling." Kili licked Ian's hand. "What happened?"

"I had no idea at first," said Sara. "But then I found an empty box of chocolates on the floor."

"Isn't chocolate poisonous for dogs?"

"Very." She wiped her eyes. "I had them on the kitchen table and didn't think she would pay attention to them. I was wrong." She shook her head in disgust. "I tried getting her to come inside the house so I could take her to the animal hospital but she didn't want to. I even used her special trigger word for the treats but it didn't work. She keeps pacing back and forth on the cement like a tiger in a zoo. That's why I came to get you. Please help me, we need to do something."

Ian caressed the side of Sara's arm. "Don't worry, we're going to get her some help. Get the leash."

"Okay."

Sara went inside to get the leash. Ian wasn't going to let anything happen to Kili. He'd carry her all the way to the hospital on his back if he had too, but he was hoping for a much easier way.

Ian got on his knees and was face to face with Kili. "Listen, you. Your mom is worried sick. We need to get you to the doctor, okay?"

Kili licked Ian on the side of his face all the way up to his ear.

Ian winced and wiped the slobber off with his forearm. "That was uncalled for." Kili licked the side of Ian's neck. "Okay, you're not listening to me. Can you pay attention so I can—" Kili licked him right across the mouth. "Yuck!" He wiped his mouth. "No disrespect to you but I prefer your mother's kisses. Got it? Now, if you don't stop that I'm not coming over anymore."

Ian stood up and walked back into Sara's home. Kili followed him.

Sara stood there in the family room with the leash in her hand and her mouth open. She pointed at Kili. "Oh my God, she followed you inside! How did you do that?"

Ian glanced down at Kili, who licked his hand. "I have no idea." Ian thought of Billy's special cologne with the pheromones.

Must be still in my system.

Ian eyed the leash in Sara's hand and held out his hand to her. "Let me see that."

Sara handed him the leash.

"Okay," said Ian, putting the leash around Kili's neck. "Come on, Kili. We need to get you some help."

Kili followed Ian through the townhome and out the front door, Sara trailing right behind them.

Sara sniffled. "You're like the Dog Whisperer."

"That was just a coincidence," said Ian. He pointed to his car on the street. "I'll drive."

Ian was just as surprised as Sara that Kili followed him to the car—it was easier than he thought it would be. He opened the back hatch of his SUV and pointed to the inside. "Okay, Kili, get in."

Kili just stood there and stared at him.

Ian turned to Sara. "Do you have special command for her to get in the car?"

Sara nodded. "Up, Kili!" Kili just stared at Sara. She tried again. "Up!"

Nothing.

Ian scratched the side of his face. "Okay. I have an idea that will either make me look like an idiot or a genius. I'm hoping for the latter." Ian crawled inside the back hatch of his SUV and scooted all the way against the backseat. Then he slapped the floor. "Come on, Kili. Up!" Kili jumped into the back of the SUV and plopped down, practically on top of Ian. "God, you weigh a ton."

Sara screamed with joy. "Yes!"

"Hang on," said Ian, fishing for the keys in his pocket. Not easy when a two-hundred pound dog is smashing the hell out of you. He finally was able to pull the keys out and handed them to Sara. "Looks like you're driving."

"Okay," said Sara, closing the hatch and running to the driver's door to get in.

Ian stroked Kili on the side of her body. "You're going to be okay, girl." He cranked his neck around toward Sara. "There's an animal hospital around the corner."

"I know exactly where it is," said Sara.

Three minutes later they arrived at the animal hospital and took Kili inside. Sara and Ian followed one of the staff members directly into the examination room where the doctor was waiting.

The doctor first asked about Kili's health history and then checked her vital signs. "How long ago did she eat the chocolate?"

"Maybe four or five hours ago, I'm guessing."

"Good. And you're sure it was chocolate and not something else?"

"I have an empty box to prove it."

"Milk chocolate? Dark? Semi—"

"Dark chocolate."

The doctor scribbled a few things on a chart. "Okay,

then. I need to induce vomiting. It's a simple procedure and I don't foresee any complications, so you two hang right here and I'll be back in just a little bit."

"Thank you, doctor."

The doctor put the leash back around Kili's neck to lead her out of the examination room, but she didn't budge. The doctor chuckled. "I didn't anticipate the complication of getting her to leave the room."

"Oh," said Ian. "I may be able to help." Ian grabbed the leash from the doctor. "Come on, Kili."

Kili followed Ian and the doctor out the door.

"Be right back," Ian told Sara from the hallway.

A minute later, Ian returned to the examination room and found Sara seated, rocking back and forth. She wiped her eyes. It was obvious how much she loved Kili—like she was her own child.

Ian sat next to Sara and wrapped his arms around her, pulling her closer to comfort her. "Hey, hey. Kili's going to be okay." He stroked Sara's hair and kissed her on the top of her head. "Remember? The doctor said he didn't expect any complications. He's probably treated something like this a thousand times."

Sara nodded. "Yeah."

"Let's focus all of our thoughts and energy on Kili coming out of there happy and healthy, looking for cookies."

Sara smiled. "Good idea. Thank you." She nodded her head a few times. "She's going to be fine."

Fifteen minutes later the doctor returned with Kili. Sara and Ian both sprang to their feet.

"All done," said the doctor. "I gave her some activated charcoal to help absorb the chocolate that already made it into her intestines. But she's going to be fine. She already looks better."

"Great!" said Ian. He smiled and felt a little emotional. That's exactly what he wanted to hear.

"Thank you!" Sara bent over and kissed Kili on the top of her head. "How's my big girl? Better now?" Sara let out a deep breath and tears streamed down her face. She turned and fell into Ian's open arms. "Thank you." She pulled away slightly to look him in the eyes and her gaze dropped to his mouth.

Was she going to kiss him? *Bring it on!* His gaze dropped to her lips.

The doctor cleared his throat. "Chocolate and dogs obviously don't mix. It can even be fatal."

Sara pulled away from Ian and sighed. "I know, I know. I thought the chocolate was out of her reach." She wiped her eyes. "She likes to eat things."

The doctor laughed. "It's not that uncommon, but everything turned out okay today. Next time she might not be so lucky, so please be careful."

"Thank you," said Sara. "I'll be extra careful."

The doctor gave Sara a few instructions and pamphlets on Kili's condition and told her what to expect over the next forty-eight hours. Then she paid the bill and they headed out.

Ian and Sara arrived back home a few minutes later. After getting Kili out from the back Ian pointed to his front door. "Come in for a beer."

Sara stared at the door for a few moments. "Probably not a good idea. And I don't want to leave Kili alone."

"Beer has *always* been a good idea, ever since it was invented back in the…" He scratched his chin. "Okay, I was trying to think of something clever to say but I drew a blank. Come inside. With Kili. It's just a beer. Plus, I want to show you something special."

She hesitated. "Just one beer."

*****

Sara followed Ian into his home and looked around.

Very impressive.

The guy had taste when it came to decorating. No black or gray colors, like what most guys gravitated towards. Most of the decor was earth tones and pastels. It almost looked like the work of a woman. Considering he's an art teacher, it shouldn't surprise her so much.

Kili laid down on the floor in Ian's family room and closed her eyes.

The poor girl must be so tired from all of the excitement.

Sara continued to inspect the place. Clean, too. She

figured that a guy who was always spilling things and opening the door while he was covered in mud would be living in a dump. Not at all. Ian's place was spotless. And he couldn't have anticipated her coming there so she had to assume that it was always like this.

"You have this surprised look on your face," said Ian, chuckling. He grabbed two beers out of the refrigerator. He opened them and handed one to her. "I can't make it out." He tapped his bottle against hers and took a sip. "But it looks like surprise."

Sara smiled. "Your place is nice. And clean."

Ian laughed. "Not what you were expecting?"

Sara shrugged. Best to not say anything. She laughed and took another sip of her beer.

"Guys have a reputation—I get it," he said. "Okay, follow me. I want to show you what's been waking you up in the mornings."

"Darn. I should have brought a sledgehammer."

He laughed and grabbed her free hand, leading her down the hallway. They passed a ceramic sculpture of a dog on the mantel and she yanked his arm back, pulling him to a dead stop.

"What?" he said.

"I'm sensing a story here," said Sara, pointing to the dog.

"You're a wise woman."

"Childhood dog?" she asked, smiling and noticing Ian's signature on the bottom of the sculpture.

"My best friend, Bailey." He winked at her.

Sara smiled, remembering she told Ian that Kili was her baby. She eyed the Australian Shepherd with the bobbed tail and gray, black, and white coat. Her blue eyes matched Ian's.

Ian pointed at the piece. "She was one of those Velcro dogs, always at my hip. And a Frisbee champion."

Sara nodded and smiled. "Must have been fun for a kid."

"The best."

"What happened?"

"Nothing bad. She had a good life—sixteen years. It was just past her time and she died in her sleep. I cried for days."

Sara tried but couldn't picture Ian crying. He always seemed so confident and strong. But it's tough to go through that—didn't matter if you're a kid or an adult.

"Sorry." She thought about Kili. St. Bernards had an average lifespan of only eight to ten years and Kili just turned seven. It was possible that she only had another year with her. Hell, today could have been her last day. Thank God it was nothing too serious at the animal hospital today. Thank God Ian was around to help.

"Hey," said Ian, pulling her close. "You okay?"

Sara wiped her eyes and forced a smile. "Life is short. Even shorter for animals."

"Yeah," he said, running his fingers through her hair. "We have to enjoy every minute while we have it."

She nodded, eyeing his lips.

God, I want to kiss you but I can't—I said I was only coming in for a beer. Uh oh, he's looking at my lips. Don't do that.

Ian moved closer and bent down to kiss her on the lips but she held up her bottle and beer-blocked him. He felt his front teeth to confirm they were still intact and blew out a deep breath. "You drive me crazy, you know that?"

"Me?" she said, playing dumb.

"I'm a guy and things need to be spelled neatly, clearly, and slowly." He looked her in the eyes and sighed. "You and I have some serious chemistry going on. Tell me why you're avoiding it."

She exhaled, trying to think of something to say.

"And that's not all," he said. "You told Becky you wanted nothing to do with me and you gave her permission to call me. I don't want to go out with her. I want to go out with you."

He stood there waiting for an answer, looking sincere and confused. Couldn't blame the poor guy; she was sending mixed signals.

"I..." She took a sip of her beer, feeling a thousand butterflies in her stomach. "It's just..." She took another sip. "Okay, I'm going to tell you, but not like this. I need to finish this beer. That will get me loopy and then I'll be able to spill the beans."

"Drunk with one beer?"

"Yes, so show me what you want to show me and then I'll tell you what's in my head."

"Promise?"

"Promise."

Ian smiled. "Follow me, then."

They entered his studio in the spare bedroom and he pointed to the potter's wheel. "First of all, this is the alligator I have been wrestling with, as you say. Public enemy number one."

Sara's gaze dropped to the potter's wheel. "This is what makes that awful noise?"

He laughed and held up his index finger. "Careful, you'll hurt her feelings." He pointed to the pieces of the lighthouse on the drying board. "And *that* is the lighthouse I'm building for my grandparent's anniversary."

"Oh…" She moved a little bit closer, inspecting the pieces. "It's going to be beautiful. And it looks like it's almost done."

"Almost. I need to reheat it to melt the glaze."

She looked around the room. "Where's the kiln?"

"In the garage."

She eyed the parts of the lighthouse again and then turned to Ian. "Your grandparents are going to love it."

What a sweet man.

She had a funny feeling in her belly—like she could trust Ian. No way could a guy who was doing something so kind for his grandparents be bad. Did she have feelings for him? Yes. And they were getting stronger by the minute.

He stood there, silent—she could tell he was waiting for her to speak.

"Thanks for sharing this with me," she said.

"You're the only one who's seen it other than my best friend Billy. Who, by the way, at this very moment is with Becky at his house."

"What? No way! What are they doing there?"

Ian laughed. "I'm not sure, but I wouldn't be surprised if she was covered in ranch dressing. Let's sit down and I'll tell you what happened. And then you'll tell me *your* story."

"Okay."

Sara followed Ian to the family room.

Was she going to tell him she had a bad experience with a past neighbor and there was no way she would go through that again? It's not like she wasn't tempted. She had strong feelings for Ian. Truth be told, she could easily fall in love with a guy like that. She was positive he had feelings too—he'd already mentioned their chemistry, which was undeniable. She buried the thoughts and sat on the couch next to Ian in the family room. She wanted to relax and not think so much. She was tired of thinking.

"Okay, the quick version," said Ian. "Becky and I went to the art exhibition as you know. Then she met Billy, they hit it off, and left me there all by my lonesome. Mind you, I had no problem with that since I didn't want to go with her in the first place."

"Then why did you agree to it?"

"This may sound lame but I didn't want to hurt her feelings."

Sweet. "It doesn't sound lame at all," she said.

"Okay, your turn," said Ian.

She took a deep breath. "Okay, I'm going to tell you why I can't go out with you."

"No thanks."

"What do you mean? I thought that's what you wanted?"

"You're not going to tell me why you can't go out with me. You're going to tell me why you *think* you can't go out with me. Then I will tell you why you're wrong."

He looked so hot with that confident grin on his face.

"That's fine," she said, then took an extra-long pull from her beer and swallowed. "Then I will tell you why you're wrong thinking I'm wrong."

He smiled again. "Good luck."

"Okay, short version too. I went out with a guy who lived next door to me. Things didn't work out and then I had to see him every day. It was awkward. Uncomfortable. So I decided to move." She swallowed hard. "So I can't go out with you because if things don't work out between us, I'll have to move away again since it would be much too painful to live next door to you."

Ian nodded and seemed to be considering what she said. "Very interesting. And how do you know things won't work out perfectly?"

She grinned. "Because I'm dealing with a man."

He pretended to pull a knife from his heart. "So cruel." They shared a good laugh together and Ian sat up. "Okay, how about if I help you with your little dating problem then?"

Sara sat up and brushed part of the couch with her hand even though it didn't need brushing. "I don't have a dating problem."

He stared at her. Even with a serious look on his face he was sexy as hell.

"You've been going out with a bunch of frogs. Time for a date with a prince."

She laughed. "You?"

He wasn't laughing and his gaze dropped to her mouth.

She couldn't help but look at his lips.

So sexy. So kissable.

They were having a mutual lip admiration moment.

"Quit looking at me that way," said Sara.

Ian grinned. "You're looking at me the same way."

It was true, but there was no way she was going to say so.

She shook her head. "What an imagination you have. Look, this isn't going to happen, you're my neighbor. I won't go through that again. I like this house."

He let out a deep breath. "At least let me go to the wedding with you as your pretend boyfriend, not as your date. Then you'd be able to stop going out with all of those freaks."

"What makes you think you'd be able to pull it off?"

"I know it would have to be the performance of my life to pretend that I like you, but I'm willing to give it a shot."

Sara smacked him on the arm.

He laughed. "I'm kidding. Besides, we can practice."

"Practice being boyfriend and girlfriend? Ha! You just want a reason to kiss me."

Not that she would mind the kissing part at all. It wasn't easy keeping him away.

Ian nodded. "I admit the thought of kissing you has crossed my mind a couple thousand times. But you need to answer this question—do you want to go to the wedding by yourself? Yes or no?"

"When you put it that way…no," she said.

"Then?"

Sara crossed her arms. "Fine. You can be my pretend boyfriend."

He grinned. "Great! Our first practice session will be tomorrow. I'm taking you to meet my grandparents. If we can convince them that we're a couple we can convince anyone."

Chapter Twelve

Ian had a rough night and didn't sleep at all. The thought of spending more time with Sara was too exciting for him to relax. A cold shower would have done him well. Fortunately, he used that time and energy to put the finishing touches on the lighthouse. It was finally done and he was thrilled with the way it turned out. The anniversary party was only two days away and he couldn't wait to give the gift to his grandparents. He was also excited to introduce Sara to them. Ian walked outside and closed the door behind him. He was immediately greeted with a heart-stopping smile from the woman who occupied his mind all night.

"Good morning," Sara said.

"Good morning to *you*," said Ian. "You almost ready?"

"Yeah." Sara gestured to Kili. "She just needs to pee and we can go." Kili sniffed around the base of the birch tree. "Which reminds me, I can't stay away too long. Her system is a little bit out of whack after what happened so she may need to poop a few more times than normal today." She cringed. "Is that too much info?"

Ian laughed. "Not at all. A dog's gotta poop."

Sara laughed. "True."

"She's feeling better?"

"Much better. Almost like new."

Kili squatted to pee. After she finished she pulled toward Ian.

"Easy!" said Sara, almost being yanked over in the process. "I told you she's got a crush on you."

Ian scratched Kili on the head and grinned. "Tell her no offense but I prefer her mother."

"We don't really need to start pretending yet," she said.

"Who says I'm pretending?"

"Knock it off."

Ian really didn't want to play pretend with Sara, but he knew it was the only way he would be able to spend time with her. For him this was real. He had strong feelings for her and wanted to be with her. The only thing he had to do was convince her that it was okay to date her neighbor. Okay to fall in love with her neighbor. Okay to live happily ever after with her neighbor.

One thing at a time…

Kili licked Ian's elbow a few times and then she turned her attention to the new plant in front of Ian's door.

"Don't worry," said Sara. "She's just sniffing a little. Then she'll find out she doesn't like it and—"

Kili opened her mouth and sucked in the plant like a Dyson vacuum cleaner.

"Kili!" yelled Sara, trying to open her giant mouth and pull the plant back out.

"Gross! I don't want it now!" said Ian, laughing. "Looks like she's *definitely* back to normal."

"Yeah," she said, laughing with Ian. "Thanks again for helping last night."

"You're welcome."

Sara put Kili back in the house and joined back up with Ian. Fifteen minutes later he pulled up to his grandparents' ranch style home in Cupertino and parked in the circular driveway.

"Hang on a second," he said, sliding out of the car and running around to the other side to open Sara's door. He extended his hand for her and she accepted it. He used his foot to push the door closed and they walked toward the house.

"Don't you think you're overdoing it?" she whispered.

He had no idea what she was talking about.

Ian squished his eyebrows together. "I haven't even done anything yet."

"Opening the door for me?"

"That wasn't part of the pretend—it's a habit. Sorry, I'll try to be a little more disrespectful in the future."

She wiggled her hand loose from his and pinched him on the side.

"Ouch!" said Ian, laughing. "Is this your idea of foreplay?"

"Shhh! Please don't embarrass me in front of your grandparents."

He shrugged his shoulders. "What? Talking about foreplay? Hey, my grandparents are the coolest and most open-minded people you'll ever meet. And they talk about sex all the time."

"Yeah right." She nudged him toward the house. "Get a move on and behave."

"Aye aye, captain."

They walked through the side gate; Ian knew he'd find them both in the garden out back.

Carl was watering and Louise was deadheading her roses.

"Hello, grandpeople," said Ian. He loved calling his grandparents that.

Louise swung around. "Hello!" She smiled and kissed Ian on the cheek. "Don't be rude—introduce us to your new girlfriend!"

Ian liked the sound of that. His girlfriend. Sara didn't even flinch at the sound of the word. He liked that too.

"Sara, these are my grandparents, Louise and Carl."

Sara extended her hand. "So wonderful to meet you."

Louise waved away her hand and extended her arms. "We're a family of huggers, so come here."

Sara's smile grew larger. "Me too, actually." She hugged Louise and Carl and then stepped back, grabbing Ian's hand again.

Carl stared at their locked hands. "How long have you two been together?"

Uh oh. They never discussed this.

"Two months," said Ian.

"Three weeks," said Sara at almost the same time.

"Four days and six hours," Ian added. "But who's counting?"

Nice recovery. Hopefully they bought it.

"Look at that!" said Louise. "They finish each other's sentences like we do! That's a—"

"Mighty good sign!" said Carl.

That was a close call. Ian hadn't thought of going over some important details ahead of time. He and Sara would definitely have to compare notes and learn a lot about each other before the wedding. But so far, so good with the grandparents. It didn't look like they had any suspicions at all and hopefully they wouldn't ask too many questions.

Ian smiled. "How are my favorite grandparents?"

Carl wagged his finger at Ian. "You'd be in serious trouble if Bill and Carol ever heard you say that."

Ian turned to Sara. "They're my other set of grandparents. I haven't seen much of them since they retired and moved to Florida. They're too busy cruising around the world to even remember they have a grandson in California."

"Don't be silly," said Louise. "We will think of you all the time when we go on our cruise to Alaska."

"If you ever go," said Ian.

Louise pointed to Carl. "He needs to get off his duff and

start looking into it."

"Don't listen to her," said Carl. "Because I never do."

"Excuse me, Carl Wilson McBride?" said Louise.

Ian laughed again.

They were entertaining when they bickered. They'd been doing it for almost fifty years.

Louise smacked Carl on the arm. "You're sleeping on the couch tonight."

"Again? One of these days I'll figure out you women." He winked and kissed Louise on the cheek.

"You think a little kiss on the cheek will get you out of the doghouse?"

"It has in the past. How about if I throw in a foot massage later on?"

"You're getting warmer."

"Fine. A foot massage *and* a back rub, but that's my final offer."

Louise smiled. "I'll take it."

Sara and Ian laughed.

"You kids hungry?" asked Louise.

"Starving," said Sara.

"Me too," said Ian.

"Great!" Louise placed some of the rose clippings in a pile and removed her gloves. "I got one of those new gadgets that makes panini sandwiches. Let's go inside."

*****

Sara was certain of one thing; Ian's grandparents were wonderful and she could see why they'd lasted fifty years together. She loved watching how they communicated, how close they were when they sat next to each other, and how Carl would caress the top of Louise's hand when she spoke. They were so affectionate considering they were most likely in their seventies. Playful too. That's how she pictured herself with her dream man in the future. Whoever that might be.

Sara glanced over at Ian. *Is it you?*

She could see by the look in Ian's eyes that he adored his grandparents. She loved that about him. There were a lot of things she loved about him, not just that he was smoking hot and a great kisser. He was kind, considerate, compassionate, an animal lover, and creative. A sense of humor was important to her and he certainly had one. In fact, Ian had everything she could ever want in a man. Too bad she couldn't date her neighbor.

The four of them were sitting at the kitchen table finishing their sandwiches and drinking lemonade when Carl jumped up from the table and moved down the hallway.

"Where are you off to in such a hurry?" asked Louise. "Is the prune juice kicking in?"

"It's a surprise," he yelled, from another room. "And the effects of the prune juice were alleviated over two hours ago!"

"Too much information!" said Ian, laughing.

Carl returned a few seconds later cupping something in his right hand. Sara, Ian, and Louise all sat quietly, watching him. Sara saw the sparkle in Carl's eye and the grin on his face and wondered what he was up to. She had no idea but she loved the mystery and the anticipation.

He kept his hand closed like a fist and placed it palm up in the middle of the table. "I wanted to share something with you." He smiled at Ian. "You have been seeing this lovely Sara for two months now. I can see you two have something special and that is wonderful."

Ian turned and smiled at Sara, kissing her on the cheek. It felt so intimate and so sweet—almost like it wasn't pretend.

"We were like you after two months of dating and look where we are now," added Carl.

"Get to the point," said Louise. "My panini is getting cold and you know how bloated I get when I eat cold cheese."

"You can sip on a cup of peppermint tea when you're done eating or stick a sock in it right now. Take your pick." He gave her a smile after she started tapping her fingers on the table. "My love."

"That will cost you another foot massage tomorrow."

"For you, the universe. Can I finish?"

"Please do."

Carl turned to Ian. "Anyway, your grandmother gave me this gift over fifty years ago and I have treasured it ever since." He opened his hand and smiled. Sitting on his palm was a tan heart-shaped rock with both of their names written on top separated by a heart.

Sara had to fight to hold back the tears. It was the sweetest thing.

Louise raised her hand to her chest. "You still have that thing? I thought you lost it years ago!"

"Never," he said, placing his hand over hers and kissing her on the cheek. "I love you forever."

Louise smiled. "I love you longer."

This is such a romantic moment.

Ian leaned over and kissed Sara on the cheek.

Wait, what is he doing? Taking advantage of the situation. You can't kiss a girl when she's vulnerable like this. I'll just want more!

"I guess I can share something too!" said Louise, standing up. She grabbed a box that was sitting on the coffee table in the living room and brought it to kitchen. "Your grandfather finally cleaned out the attic last week and found some things I haven't seen in decades. This is one of them." She smiled and opened the box, pulling a small ceramic owl from it.

Ian pointed to the owl. "Did Uncle Steven make that?"

Louise shook her head. "Your father did."

He cocked his head to the side and held out his hand. Louise handed the owl to Ian and he checked it out. He glanced back over to his grandmother. "Really?"

"Of course! He gave it to me."

Ian's father was obviously talented. Ian hadn't mentioned

that. He talked more about his Uncle Steven and how world-renowned he was. He really seemed to be inspecting the owl, deep in thought.

"I don't get it," said Ian.

"What don't you get?" asked Carl.

"He never showed me any of his work and he told me he wasn't good enough to sculpt for a living. This here is just as good as Uncle Steven's. Maybe even better."

"I agree," said Carl. "Your father had plenty of talent and he had the passion for it. But he had to make a choice and decided to take the safer route, as he calls it. To provide for you and your mother."

"He never told me that."

Carl nodded. "Not a surprise. I think he changed a lot after he made that decision. Like he lost that spark or something."

It didn't sound like Ian and his father had a close relationship. Sara wanted to hug Ian but would he think the hug was pretend or from the heart? It would definitely be from the heart.

"I personally think he could have done both," said Louise. "But he didn't want to consider it because he was too stubborn. Wonder where he got that from?" She pretended to knock on Carl's head.

"Hey!" said Carl.

Ian and Sara laughed.

"I thought you wanted to follow in his footsteps," said

Carl.

Ian shook his head. "He convinced me to take the safer route like he did but I wanted to open up a gallery." He looked even deeper in thought. "Still do."

Carl slapped Ian on the back. "It's not too late. I guess you were supposed to see this owl to light a fire under your butt. Life is short. You've got to live while you've got life in you."

Ian nodded and smiled. "You're right, Grandpa. Thank you."

"I didn't do anything! Now, I'll tell you what I *will* do, I'll help you find that gallery. I may be retired but my real estate license is still good. I'll even invest in the property if you'll let me."

"That's an amazing offer. Why wouldn't I let you?"

Carl shrugged. "Some people don't like handouts."

"It would be an investment and I have no problem with it at all. Let me think about that."

"Great! Then you can start living your passion!"

Sara could see Ian's energy level shoot up—like he had a shot of espresso. That's all most people need, someone to believe in them.

Sara leaned in to get a closer look at the ceramic owl. She loved the intricate details of the feathers and the big yellow eyes.

"It's beautiful," said Sara.

"Let me see it," said Louise, holding out her hand.

"There's something even more beautiful inside that I want to show you." Ian handed her the owl and she removed the head from the owl and set it on the table. She reached in and pulled out a piece of paper, carefully unfolding it. "Your grandfather wrote this to me the day after I gave him that rock. I haven't opened it since our silver anniversary twenty-five years ago."

"A love letter?" asked Sara.

"Even better. A love letter *proposal*."

"Let's not make a big deal about this," said Carl, shifting in his seat. "Anybody in the mood for apple pie?"

Ian turned to Carl. "You wrote down your proposal?"

Carl threw his palms in the air. "I was going to propose to the prettiest woman I had ever laid eyes on! I'm surprised I didn't wet myself."

Sara and Ian laughed.

"I didn't want to mess it up or forget something," added Carl. He turned to Sara. "We were standing in front of the lighthouse in San Simeon and it was the most *beautiful* day of the year."

Sara was dying to know what the letter said. "Please read it!"

Oops. She didn't mean to yell.

Louise laughed. "Don't mind if I do!"

"Not necessary," said Carl. "What about strawberries? Anybody in a fruity mood?"

Louise sat up straight, cleared her throat and read the

letter. "My love…please marry me." She grinned and folded the letter back up, dropped it inside the owl, and placed the owl's head back on.

Ian's head shot from Louise to Carl. "Five words? You thought you were going to forget that?"

"I was nervous!"

Louise laughed. "He wasn't a man of many words back then. Now I can't get him to shut up."

"I think it's wonderful how nervous you were," said Sara. "That shows how much you wanted her to say yes."

Carl nodded and a smile appeared on his face. "She was the only thing that mattered to me." He leaned over and kissed Louise. "Still is."

Ian reached under the table for Sara's hand and she pinched him.

"Ouch!" said Ian.

Carl raised an eyebrow. "What are you two up to?"

"She can't keep her hands off of me," said Ian. "She can get a little rough sometimes."

She was going to kill him.

Louise perked up. "A passionate woman! Nothing wrong with that at all. She sees what she likes and she goes for it!"

Not necessarily, Grandma. I like Ian and I'm definitely not going for it. I have serious issues.

"That's what attracted me to her," said Ian. "Her passion."

He leaned over and kissed her on the lips and held it

there for a few seconds.

She pulled away after she remembered where she was. She felt a little dizzy but she needed to speak to Ian and now! Sara pointed to the dishes on the table. "Ian…darling. Help me bring the dishes to the kitchen, please."

"Leave everything here!" said Louise. "I'll take care of that later."

"No, no," said Sara. "Ian and I have a rule."

"What rule?" asked Ian.

She reached under the table again and pinched him.

"Ouch!" he yelled again.

"Men," said Sara. "Always forgetful."

"Tell me about it," said Louise. "Now you know why Carl had to write the proposal down! But what can we do?"

Sara chuckled. "Accept it—that's all we can do. Anyway, the rule is whoever doesn't cook has to clean up. No argument." She gave Ian a stern look. "Honey, grab the other plates."

"Yes, dear."

Loaded with plates, Sara and Ian headed to the kitchen.

After placing the plates in the sink Sara poked Ian in the chest. "What are you doing?"

"What?"

"You know what!" she said, trying to keep her voice down. "I don't like this game we're playing…it's confusing me. I don't want to pretend anymore."

"Fine. I'll be your real boyfriend then."

"No! That's not what I'm saying. Okay, we'll talk about this later. But for now, please stop kissing me!"

In her peripheral Sara saw a body and turned. Louise. Wide-eyed with her mouth open.

Uh oh. Think!

Sara grabbed the neckline of Ian's shirt and pulled him close. "Did you hear me? Stop kissing me *unless* you're going to kiss me with passion!"

She yanked his head down and planted her lips on his. It only took a second before Ian reciprocated and pulled her in closer. Their lips and bodies felt so wonderful together. They were connected. These kisses with Ian were magical. She wanted a thousand of them. No. A billion!

"I really like this woman, Ian!" said Louise. "You picked yourself a winner. I hope you're bringing her to the anniversary party."

Ian pulled away from the kiss. "Wow."

Sara loved the way Ian was looking at her. It was the same way Carl looked at Louise. With love and tenderness.

It sure didn't seem like he was pretending. If he was, he was *really* good.

Ian turned to his grandmother. "Did you say something, Grandma?"

"Yes." She pointed to Sara. "Make sure you bring this woman to the party. I won't take no for an answer."

Chapter Thirteen

Sara felt refreshed and full of energy the next morning. She enjoyed a cup of coffee in the kitchen, thinking of her sexy neighbor. He had invaded her dreams practically all night long.

She enjoyed spending time with Ian and his grandparents. Carl and Louise were wonderful. She was looking forward to seeing them again tomorrow at the anniversary party. And seeing Ian. Just the thought of the man brought the butterflies back to her stomach.

"I don't know if I should be doing this, Kili."

Kili didn't acknowledge her comment and continued to nap on the kitchen floor by her feet.

Sara went to the family room in the front of the house, flipping open the plantation shutters and admiring the blue sky. She slid open the window and could hear the birds singing this morning. She smiled and took a deep breath. What a beautiful day.

"Thanks, you're the best," said a female voice.

Sara leaned forward and turned her gaze toward Ian's door—a woman was leaving.

What the…

She felt her blood pressure rising, watching the hair-flipping-giggly-jiggly-barely-eighteen-girl-woman-thing walk to the street and get in her bright red Volkswagen Bug convertible. It was the same girl Ian was with last week at Orchard Valley Coffee.

Did she spend the night?

She paced back and forth in her living room. Just when she was letting down her guard this happened. How could he? She was pissed off and there was no way she was going to stand for this. Time to give Ian a piece of her mind.

Who does he think he is?

"Kili, time to go potty!"

Kili woke up and came running to the entryway. Sara wrapped the collar around her neck, grabbed the leash, and patted the dog on the head. Kili was the only one she could trust, the only one who was one hundred percent loyal. Always.

Kili peed at the base of what was now her favorite tree—the birch—and Sara led her to Ian's door. She knocked and waited, staring at the dirt in the planter box below her. No way was she going to replace that plant again after what Ian did.

Ian opened the door and grinned at Sara. "Good morning, beautiful." Kili pulled toward Ian and licked his hand. "Yes, I think you're beautiful too, Kili." Ian laughed but then cut it short, obviously seeing the expression on Sara's face. "You okay?"

"We need to talk," said Sara.

"Of course," said Ian. "Come in!"

Sara and Kili followed Ian inside toward the kitchen.

Stay calm and speak your mind.

Ian pointed proudly to the lighthouse sitting on top of cardboard on the kitchen table. "It's done! I'm going to take it over to Villa Ragusa to set it up. It will be on display on the middle of the dance floor during the cocktail hour and the dinner."

"It's amazing. But I thought the party was tomorrow."

"It is, but the catering director said I could come by today since the banquet room wasn't being used for an event."

She nodded. It didn't really matter since she wasn't going to the event now. No way.

Don't delay this.

"Is there something you want to tell me?" she asked.

Ian stood there with a dumb look on his face. "Not that I know of."

Nice try. You deserve an Oscar for your performance.

"Nothing at all?" she asked. "Maybe something you did recently behind my back?"

Ian broke eye contact with Sara and shifted his weight from one leg to the other. "Oh. That."

"Yes. That."

He blew out a breath. "Okay, yes, I admit it. I called Daniel."

"Excuse me?"

"I told him to stay away from you, so—"

Sara threw up her hand. "Wait a minute! You're talking about Daniel? Daniel, the guy I went out with?"

"Of course, who else?"

She felt her pulse pounding in her head. Daniel was the only one out of the bunch that wasn't a frog. He was a decent man. Now it made sense why he send that email! How dare Ian get involved in her personal life? And he told Daniel to stay away from her?

"Why the hell did you tell him to stay away from me?" she asked.

"Because he's married."

"He's—" She felt her left eye twitch. "What do you mean he's married?"

"It's self-explanatory."

It can't be.

Sara felt some nausea coming on and tried to regain her composure. She took a deep breath. Good, the twitching stopped. "Okay, what makes you think he's married? Explain."

"I don't *think* he's married. I *know* he is. He's the father of one of my students."

"Unbelievable! Why didn't you tell me you did this?"

"For fear of you reacting the way you're reacting right now. But I don't see what the big deal is. Do you *like* to go out with married men?"

"Of course not! What a ridiculous question. And how about I throw a question your way? Do you *like* to sleep with women half your age? Don't answer that! The answer is obvious since I saw one of them leave your house!"

Sara didn't like this conversation any longer, but what she hated even more was the way Ian was looking at her. As if *she* was the one who did something wrong.

"You don't know me at all, do you?" he asked with a look of disgust.

"I guess not."

Ian ran a hand through his hair. "I'll tell you one thing, jealousy doesn't look good on you. That expression you have on your face—I had to live with that look on the face of my father every single day as I grew up. That look makes my stomach turn. Look, I'm sorry I told Daniel to take a hike. Yeah, there was probably a better way I could have handled that—maybe I should have told you and let you deal with it. But the guy was a loser so I did what I did."

She folded her arms. "Well, it wasn't right."

"I'm sorry. That's one thing. But then you come in here and accuse me of sleeping with students I'm tutoring? *That* hurts me—"

What is he talking about? "You tutor?"

Ian threw his palms in the air. "I thought I told you. I tutor French on the side. You've seen me at Orchard Valley Coffee with a couple of my students, remember?"

"Students?"

"Yes—students! Not that I have to tell you but I haven't had sex in over two years. And who are you to judge me? Look at you—you went out with a married man! And *you* need to take a fake date to a wedding to try to impress someone you don't even talk to anymore when I'm absolutely positive that most men would *kill* to go out with you. When you're not acting like a damn fool, that is. Sex with my student? The truth is, she came by this morning to borrow a book in French that I recommended. She also brought a thank you gift from her parents." He pointed to the plate covered with plastic wrap on the kitchen counter.

Sara felt like a complete idiot. The girls she was jealous over were just students of Ian's. She went out with a married man. And to top it off, she had been preventing herself from going out with her neighbor who was always keeping her out of trouble. How could this get any worse?

She stared at the plate on the counter that was filled with her favorite treats. She shook her head, embarrassed. "Chocolate chip cookies."

Kili jumped up and rammed into the kitchen table hard.

Sara watched—in what seemed like slow motion—as the lighthouse fell over and rolled off the table, slamming into the floor and shattering.

"No!" yelled Ian, lunging for it but not in time.

Sara raised her hand to her chest. She was speechless.

Nothing was going to fix this situation. Nothing.

She took a deep breath and closed her eyes. When she

opened them she would realize this was all a bad dream. She took another deep breath and then opened her eyes.

Damn! Not a dream. And Ian looked even more pissed off than before.

He pointed toward the front door, his breathing heavy and his face red. "You and that dog of yours, get out of here."

"Please let me—"

"Now!"

Chapter Fourteen

Two hours later Sara had run out of tears. She called Becky, completely distraught. She had to do *something* after that disaster at Ian's house but she couldn't think straight.
She needed someone to do the thinking for her.

Fortunately, after fifteen minutes on the phone with Becky, they had come up with a decent plan that would fix at least part of the situation. Ian had told Sara there was a replica of the same lighthouse at a gallery in Cambria, a town about three hours south of Campbell. She had located the gallery online and called them to confirm that they still had the lighthouse. Luckily they still had it and she paid for it with a credit card over the phone to make certain nobody else bought it. Sara and Becky were now in the car driving south on Highway 101 headed to pick it up.

"Please change the station before I hurl myself out the window." said Sara.

The last thing she really needed was to listen to the theme from *Titanic*. Although the song fit she felt like she was sinking deeper and deeper with every dumb move she made.

"I've got a better idea," said Becky, turning off the radio.

Sara covered her mouth with her hand and mumbled,

"Oh God."

"What?" asked Becky, who glanced over and then got her eyes back on the road.

"I realized I'm going to have to move again."

"Don't be so dramatic, he'll get over it."

"No way. You didn't see his face. In just one look I saw pity, sadness, hurt, anger, and disgust. I think I even saw homicide."

Becky laughed. "That was his testosterone kicking in. Once he has time to calm down and analyze what happened, he'll realize that this was all a big misunderstanding and that the lighthouse thing was an accident. He'll forgive you—especially after you deliver the new lighthouse."

"The new lighthouse will be only a band-aid over the wound. The scar will always be there. How could I let this happen again?"

"I don't know. You never told me what happened the first time with Brian."

That's because I'm an expert at changing the subject. "You hungry? We should stop for a pee break and a snack."

"Nice try, but it's not going to work this time. Unless you want me to put on some depressing music." Becky reached for the radio and grinned. "Let's see what we can find…"

Sara pushed her hand away. "Don't you dare." She had never told anyone what happened with her ex, Brian. But Becky was helping her today and she was trapped in her car so she couldn't avoid the topic this time.

Sara signed. "I'm going to try to do this in one breath so I can get it over as quickly as possible. Hopefully I don't throw up."

Becky laughed. "Good luck."

Sara took in a big breath. "Brian told me he needed space, that he wasn't ready for marriage, so he broke up with me. The prick immediately started dating a woman ten years younger than me, and got engaged to her after three weeks. They got married, she moved in next door, she got pregnant. All of this happened within six months of our breakup."

"What a dickish bastard."

She nodded. "I couldn't handle seeing them together every day, not to mention hearing certain disgusting things through the walls. So I moved to Campbell where I obviously did not learn my lesson, because I quickly developed the hots for my next door neighbor again. Then I saw Ian with a few girls half his age and thought it was happening to me all over again. I freaked."

"You should tell this to Ian so he can see that you had a little baggage from your last relationship. He seems like a smart guy and will understand why you jumped to conclusions. We also have our hormones and he needs to understand that."

Sara wasn't even listening to Becky. She pictured Ian's face again, looking down at the broken pieces of the lighthouse on the floor. And the way he looked at her when he spoke to her.

You and that dog of yours, get out of here.

He had every right to kick them out. She didn't think she would ever be able to forgive herself for what she had done to him so why would she expect him to do the same? And even if he did, there was still the problem of him being her neighbor.

Sara sighed. "It doesn't really matter. Yes, I hope he forgives me but we can't see each other. There's too much risk of pain. I have feelings for him but look at me after our first squabble. I'm a mess. Imagine if I was deeply in love with the guy and this happened. I don't even want to think about it!"

Becky laughed. "It's obvious you've already fallen for him. Big time!"

Sara raised an eyebrow and turned to Becky. "Have not."

"Uh huh…"

Had she? She'd better not have! She needed to put some space in between her and Ian immediately before it was too late.

"There's only one thing I can do," said Sara.

"Have sex with him?"

"No! I'm not going to have sex with him. I'm going to do the opposite."

"Let him have sex with you?"

"No!"

"Have sex with yourself?"

"God, no. Am I the only one listening to me? No sex. Not with him. Not with myself. I need to get out of town."

"You can't be serious! You can't run away from your problems."

"Watch me. And please let me do it. My head is going to explode."

"Okay, okay. I'm not going to say anything else. But I think you're making a mistake."

"Maybe I am—we'll find out soon enough. I'm going to deliver the lighthouse and then get away to the coast for a while to clear my head. I know the perfect place and I can bring Kili with me. Being near the beach in Carmel with a bottle of wine, or three, and a few romance novels always does me good."

Becky slapped the steering wheel. "Speaking of which, Billy did me good last night."

"You slut!"

"That's me! I couldn't help myself—the man's intelligence is a serious turn-on. In fact, the scientist part of his brain invented a couple of new sexual positions. He tested one of them out on me last night. He named it the Bavarian Wheelbarrow."

"I don't want to know."

"Fab-u-lous."

Sara pointed to Becky's hairless arms.

"Has Billy been experimenting on you recently?"

Becky lit up. "Almost every day! There's nothing that my

Billy can't do—the man's a genius. He calls me his favorite guinea pig."

"And you *like* that?"

"Yes!"

They both had a good laugh, which was what Sara really needed. They picked up the lighthouse at the gallery in Cambria without a hitch and drove directly to Villa Ragusa to set it up. Then she packed up a few things, along with Kili, and headed to Carmel.

It would have been nice to have been at the anniversary party to see the expression on Carl and Louise's faces when they saw the lighthouse. It would have been wonderful to celebrate with them and have another dance with Ian. And a few of those amazing kisses too. But it wasn't going to happen. She needed to forget about him because there was no way he would forgive her.

*****

"Excuse me?" said Ian, certain he had heard the gallery owner, Krasimir, incorrectly. It sounded like he said he had sold the lighthouse. Ian scanned the gallery again but it was nowhere to be found.

"I'm so sorry," said Krasimir. "I sold it literally an hour ago. I was wondering when I would sell it, then out of nowhere, *two* people want to buy it on the same day. This is amazing."

Not amazing. More like a nightmare.

Ian was totally screwed. Things kept getting worse and worse. He thought he had the perfect plan to salvage the fiasco his neighbor created this morning. It hadn't occurred to him to call Krasimir ahead of time to make sure he still had the piece before driving over three hours to Cambria.

Ian paced back and forth in front of Krasimir. "What am I going to do now?"

"You'll figure something out. These things happen for a reason and I'm sure everything will turn out fine. In the meantime, I can offer you an espresso or a latte if you'd like."

Ian scanned the gallery again. "Here?"

Krasimir chuckled. "Yes. I have an espresso machine in the back for my customers."

A latte sounded good and he could use a little caffeine for the drive back. "A latte would be great, thank you. With a couple of sugars."

Krasimir smiled. "You got it. I'll be right back."

Ian wandered around the gallery admiring the statues, figurative sculptures, colorful bird houses, and decorative pottery. He loved the way Krasimir had everything displayed and the man was obviously a talented potter and sculptor.

That feeling in Ian's gut returned, the one that told him he should have his own gallery. It made his heart race, but the anxiety he was feeling was positive, not negative. Like it was the right thing to do. His father had given up his dream —his passion—but that didn't mean Ian had to do the same.

An older couple entered the gallery and closed the door behind them.

The man smiled at Ian. "We want to take a peek at something we saw through the window."

Funny. The guy thought Ian was the owner. That felt great.

Ian smiled back. "Krasimir will be right back if you have any questions about the pieces."

"Thank you," said the man.

The woman eyed a tall gallon-sized ceramic jug with a green handle and ran her fingers over the pattern of four leaf clovers on the side of it. She turned back to Ian and pointed to the jug. "I love this. How did you create these patterns on the side? I've taken a few pottery classes but this can't be easy."

Ian glanced back to find Krasimir but he was still in the back at the espresso machine. He cleared his throat. "This is not my piece, but most likely Krasimir used an adhesive vinyl stencil and then glazed over it."

"That is correct," said Krasimir, returning from the back room. He handed Ian his latte and smiled. "I used a brush for the glazing instead of dipping it. Then I used an X-acto knife to lift off the remaining vinyl pieces once the glaze was dry."

"It's absolutely beautiful." The woman flipped the tag over to view the price and nodded. "I'll take it."

Ian smiled. He had helped Krasimir sell one of his

pieces.

What an exhilarating feeling. And he knew the feeling would be magnified by at least a hundred if he were selling his own creations. He took a deep breath and exhaled, a smile forming on his face.

Krasimir wrapped the jug carefully in paper and placed it in a box for the couple. After they left, he smiled at Ian. "Thanks for your help, I appreciate it."

"My pleasure. I love your gallery. Business is good?"

"It's great. I get a steady stream of tourists coming in here all year long. Most of them are in the area to visit Hearst Castle in San Simeon." He looked around the gallery. "Sometimes I wish I had a little more space, but I can't complain at all."

"How come you don't get a larger place?"

"Commercial properties are scarce in a small town of only six thousand people. Actually, I have been toying with the idea of opening a second gallery out where you are in Silicon Valley and then having someone manage this one."

This conversation was getting interesting. "Where?"

"Not sure yet, but I need to jump on it. My wife was offered a job at Apple."

"She already accepted the job?"

"Not yet. She's waiting on me to figure out what I want to do with this gallery. The job she was offered is a high-level dream job that most people would kill to have, but she wants me to be happy too."

"Sounds like a sweet woman. And smart."

Ian had the urge to tell Krasimir about his dreams of having his own gallery but the words of his father echoed in his head.

Teaching is safe and the safe route is the smart route. Anything else is foolish.

Then he remembered what Sara had said when they shared a beer that night at her place.

Sometimes you just have to go for what you want.

He liked her advice better. And she was right. Why not go for it? He was tired of being scared. And even more tired of his dad's discouraging remarks.

Ian was going to throw it out there to Krasimir, he had nothing to lose. "I've been thinking of opening a gallery too, maybe even with enough space to offer pottery classes."

"Is that right?"

Ian nodded. "Maybe we should team up." He pulled the iPhone from his pocket and went to his photo albums. Then he handed the phone to Krasimir. "Swipe to the left and you can see some of my work."

Krasimir went through the photos, nodding. "Very nice." He looked at a few more photos. "I must say, I'm impressed." He handed the phone back to Ian.

"Thank you. I'm passionate about my work and it's obvious you are too. We should chat about this—I mean, if you'd be open to the possibility of having a partner."

Say yes.

Krasimir shrugged. "Probably not the best idea."

At least I tried.

"How do you think my ego would feel after all of your pieces sold before mine?" asked Krasimir, looking like he was holding back a laugh. He slapped Ian on the back. "That's a compliment!"

Ian let out a deep breath. "Thank you."

Krasimir chuckled. "I was online last night looking at the real estate market in your area. It's insane, so I'd definitely be open to chatting about a partnership. Especially with someone who does work of your caliber."

"Great!"

They agreed to talk later that evening on the phone and meet up again soon in person.

Ian was ecstatic.

What a rollercoaster of a day and it all started with Sara this morning. Crazy, beautiful Sara.

And that's when it hit Ian. This was all meant to be. Sara was supposed to break his lighthouse. He was supposed to come to Cambria—not to buy Krasimir's lighthouse but to be in this gallery environment and see the possibilities. To *feel* them. And to chat with Krasimir, of course.

Maybe I need to thank Sara for breaking the lighthouse.

Ian chuckled at the thought. He certainly felt a lot better than he did this morning. And much better than when he found out someone else bought the lighthouse. Krasimir was right, these things happen for a reason.

"Oh man," Ian said to himself on the drive home.

With all of the excitement, Ian had completely forgotten one important detail. He didn't have a gift to give to his grandparents for their anniversary. And he had twenty-four hours to find something special. Sara was another story. After the way he yelled at her this morning, he wouldn't be surprised if she never spoke to him again.

Chapter Fifteen

The next day Ian pulled up and parked outside of Villa Ragusa for his grandparents' anniversary party. He was twenty minutes late but was having a rough day. His numerous phone calls to Sara had gone straight to her voicemail and she didn't seem to be at home the ten or twelve times he went over there to knock on her door. He wanted to apologize for yelling at her. He felt bad about that. Where was she? She was invited to the party, but he knew there was no way she would be there after what had happened.

Then there was the matter of finding a special gift for his grandparents. It took him a few hours of brainstorming and researching on the Internet, but at least he finally figured that part out. Carl and Louise always talked about going on a cruise to Alaska so he booked them on a ship that would leave in three weeks out of San Francisco.

He entered Villa Ragusa and climbed the stairs toward the ballroom. He was so looking forward to celebrating with them—fifty years married was a big deal. He hoped one day he would be celebrating the same thing.

Ian swung the door open and stepped inside the

ballroom. The atmosphere was lively, with over a hundred people laughing, smiling, and chatting up a storm during the cocktail hour. The DJ played some cool Motown music from the sixties and everyone seemed to be having a great time.

He scanned the room for his grandparents and his eyes stopped on the dance floor.

No way.

There was a lighthouse displayed on a table in the middle of the dance floor. Not the lighthouse Sara broke yesterday, obviously—that was beyond repair. It was the one from Krasimir's gallery. There were only two people who knew he was working on the lighthouse. Billy and Sara. But Sara was the only one who knew about the replica in Cambria. It was her. She was the one who bought the lighthouse from Krasimir one hour before Ian showed up! *Unbelievable.* Driving all the way to Cambria, not to mention the large sum of money she spent to make things good.

"Sara, you're an amazing woman," he said to himself, smiling. The thought of her warmed his heart. And that's when he knew. He was falling in love with her. He glanced around the room looking for the prettiest girl he'd ever met.

"Ian!" yelled Louise, walking in his direction with Carl at her side.

"Hello grandpeople!" said Ian, smiling. "Happy anniversary!"

"Thank you!" said Louise. She hugged Ian and kissed him several times, rotating back and forth from one cheek to the other. "*You* are the best grandson in the world! Thank you, thank you, thank you for the most wonderful gift. We'll cherish it always."

Ian didn't feel good about this. Sara deserved the credit and he had to say something immediately. "About that—"

"It's beautiful!" said Carl. He threw open his arms and hugged Ian. "That might be your best work ever. Is it waterproof? We can put it out in the backyard to keep the roses company."

Louise smacked Carl on the arm. "Don't be ridiculous. That is going *inside* the house."

"Fine. Then how about if we get rid of that sewing machine of yours? We can put it there."

Louise placed her hands on her hips. "Do you want to sleep on the couch on the evening of your anniversary?"

"How about a foot massage later?"

Louise kissed Carl on the cheek. "You're forgiven."

Carl placed his hand on Ian's shoulder. "These women aren't dummies, son. I'm telling you, they plan this stuff! Your grandmother here always starts with what seems like a normal conversation. Then she dangles a carrot in front of my old nose long enough for me to stick my foot in my mouth. It happens every day!"

"Grandma's a smart woman," said Ian, laughing.

Carl leaned in and whispered to Ian. "We'll let her keep thinking that. What she doesn't know is I do these things on purpose because I love giving her foot massages."

Ian laughed.

"What are you two up to?" asked Louise.

"Nothing at all," said Carl, winking at Ian. "I was asking where that lovely Sara is."

Damn. Ian was about to ask him the same question. "You haven't seen her?"

"No. We thought she'd be coming with you. That's how things are done, you know?" Carl pointed off to the side. "Even Billy brought a date but I'll tell you that woman has the weirdest laugh."

Ian cranked his head toward the bar and spotted Billy with Becky standing very close to each other. He was sure Becky would know where Sara was. But first he had to come clean with his grandparents about the lighthouse.

"Louise! Carl!" said a woman approaching his grandparents. "Happy anniversary!"

Looked like he would have to wait to talk with them. Ian worked his way over toward the bar where he waited for Billy to stop kissing Becky.

He lost his patience and finally cleared his throat. "Is this an experiment?"

Becky came up for air and laughed, sounding like a donkey in labor. "I can't seem to pull myself away from this savage."

Ian pointed to Billy's neck. "You wearing that special cologne?"

"Nah, I scrapped that experiment when the

neighborhood cats started camping out on my front porch and spraying the tires on my car. This is all natural."

"Natural, indeed," said Becky, rubbing Billy's chest. She glanced over Ian's shoulder to the dance floor and smiled. "Isn't that lighthouse amazing?"

Ian turned to take another look at the lighthouse. A few of the guests were taking selfies with it. He turned back to Becky. "Yes, it's amazing and I know Sara was the one who bought it."

"I went with her!" she said proudly. "You won't believe how much money she spent on that thing."

"I know exactly how much she spent and I'd like to know why she did it."

"Isn't it obvious?"

"I'm a man," said Ian. "I need things clearly explained. Charts and graphs would help—even better if you've got a PowerPoint presentation."

She laughed again, this time sounding more like a rabid monkey on helium. "Okay, let me say this." Her face got serious. "You would be an idiot if you let that woman go. Fight for her."

Ian grinned. "Where is she?"

"Okay, here's the thing. She kind of, sort of went away for a while."

"Graphs? Charts? Help me out here. What are you talking about?"

Becky shrugged. "She said she needed to get out of town

to clear her head. I tried to talk her out of it but she's stubborn. And *no*, I'm not going to tell you where she is."

"Do you accept bribes?"

"Nope."

"How do you respond to blackmail?"

She stared at him.

"Okay," he said. "No blackmail. At least tell me how long she'll be gone."

"That I don't know. She said she would come back when she's ready."

What the heck did that mean? Ready for what?

Ian blew out a breath. "How can I fight for her if she's not even here? God, I need a drink."

This didn't sound very promising. If Sara was truly interested in Ian she wouldn't have left town. It didn't make sense. But Becky was right—he needed to fight for her and do whatever it took to show her how much he cared.

"Friends and family," said the DJ. "Please take a seat. Dinner will be served shortly."

Ian grabbed a glass of wine from the bar and headed over to his table where his grandparents were already seated. He eyed the two empty chairs next to them and pointed to them. "Don't tell me Mom and Dad aren't going to make it."

"They missed their flight and are stuck in Rome," said Carl. "They decided since they were going to miss the party they will extend the vacation another week and head to Amsterdam."

A waiter came and placed a Caesar salad in front of each of them. The table was set for six but since Sara and Ian's parents didn't make it, it felt kind of empty with only three.

Ian couldn't believe his parents would miss the party. On the bright side, he didn't have to listen to his dad talk about how having a gallery was foolish. He smiled when he thought of his dad's face when he found out that he and Krasimir were going into business together, opening a gallery. In fact, they had plans to check out a property in downtown Campbell tomorrow. Too bad Sara wasn't there to share the news with.

"Everything okay, honey?" asked Louise, rubbing the top of Ian's hand.

Ian crinkled his nose. "Not really. I have a confession to make." He took in a deep breath and let it out slowly. "I didn't make the lighthouse."

"I know, dear."

Ian opened his mouth and then closed it. How the heck did she know?

Louise laughed and patted the top of his hand. "It wasn't that difficult to figure out considering some man named Krasimir signed his name on the base."

Ian nodded. "There's actually a second part of the confession. I didn't buy the lighthouse from Krasimir."

"You stole it?" asked Carl.

Louise shot Carl a look. "Are you seriously asking your

grandson that question? Of course he didn't steal it. He's trying to tell us that Sara bought it for us."

Ian threw his palms up in the air. "How do you know this?"

"Yeah," said Carl. "How *do* you know?"

Louise smiled. "First, I'm a woman. And also, I was here yesterday when Sara dropped it off."

Ian sat up in his seat. "You saw Sara? How did she look? Was she okay? Did she mention me?"

"Oh boy," said Carl. "Sounds like somebody's got it bad."

"Honestly?" said Louise. "She looked a little sad."

That's not what he wanted to hear. He hated to think that she was sad and he knew it was because of him. He wished she was there right now so he could hug her and say he was sorry. Instead, she left town to get away from him.

"I did make *a* lighthouse for you, but Sara's dog accidentally knocked it over and it was beyond repair. Sara felt so bad she drove over three hours each way to buy *that* one from a gallery in Cambria. She spent her own money and it wasn't cheap. I had no idea she did it until I showed up here this evening. I had already bought you a different gift."

Carl studied the lighthouse for a few seconds and then turned to Ian. "I must admit, I'm not very happy about this."

Damn. He didn't expect his grandfather to take it so bad.

"How come you haven't married that woman yet?"

asked Carl. "Sara is a gem!"

"She is!" added Louise.

Ian couldn't argue with that. One of the rarest gems in the world.

Carl waved at the DJ and stood up. "Time for a toast."

Louise smiled. "Don't torture the guests, my love. Short and sweet."

"Short and sweet," Carl repeated, kissing Louise on the cheek. "Like you."

Louise pointed at her husband. "Watch it, mister."

Carl chuckled and pulled a piece of paper out of his pocket and winked at Ian. "I wrote the toast down so I wouldn't forget."

"Why doesn't this surprise me?" said Louise.

Ian laughed. His grandparents wouldn't be the same if they weren't always arguing about something, but they didn't fool anyone. Beneath their words, beneath their arguments, beneath their threats of killing each other was a love so strong it could withstand a hurricane.

Carl took the microphone from the DJ and smiled. "I think this is a good time for a toast." He cleared his throat and unfolded the piece of paper, studying it for a moment. "Thank you for fifty years of marriage." He smiled again, folded the piece of paper, and slid it back into his pocket. The guests laughed and Carl blew kisses to them as if they were his adoring fans and had given the speech of a lifetime. He handed the microphone to the DJ and—

"You hold on one minute, Carl Wilson McBride!" said Louise. "Do you want to sleep on the couch again?"

The guests laughed again and Carl played dumb. "What did I do?"

"You know what you did—now undo it."

"Fine, fine. To be honest, I had a feeling that first toast wouldn't fly, so fortunately I have a backup plan." He got serious for a moment and pulled a scroll from his inside suit pocket. He held the scroll above his head and unrolled until the bottom smacked the floor. "Hear ye, hear ye!"

The guests cheered and applauded.

Carl cleared his throat and locked eyes with Louise. "Dear Louise. My love. The truth is we don't have enough time this evening or enough space on this scroll for me to tell you how many ways I love you." He handed the scroll off to the DJ, who moved to the side. "I don't need that—I want to speak from the heart. You mean the world to me. Always have, always will. There's not a day that goes by that I don't count my lucky stars for having you in my life." He pointed to the lighthouse in the middle of the dance floor. "I was a young fool who didn't know much of anything when I proposed to you in front of that lighthouse over fifty years ago. But I was smart enough to know that my life would have been nothing without you." He pulled a handkerchief from his pocket and wiped his eyes. "Now I'm an old fool, but my feelings haven't changed one bit. I love you from the bottom of my heart." He walked over to the table and lifted his wine glass in the direction of Louise. "To the best thing that ever happened to me. Cheers."

The room yelled together "Cheers" and applauded. Carl sat back down next to Louise and handed her his handkerchief.

She wiped her eyes. "That was beautiful, but you're still sleeping on the couch."

"Now what?"

"Do you realize what you've done to my makeup?"

Carl kissed Louise on the lips. "You look beautiful."

Ian found himself getting a little misty-eyed during the toast. They enjoyed a wonderful dinner, and later that evening Ian had the pleasure of watching his grandparents dance to the same song that was their first dance at their wedding fifty years ago. "The Way You Look Tonight" by Frank Sinatra. He loved that sparkle in their eyes as they danced together. His thoughts flashed back to the art & wine festival where he shared that dance with Sara.

What a dance. What a kiss.

The only thing that would have made the anniversary party more complete was the presence of Sara. He had no idea how long she would be gone, but he was certain even a day without her would feel like an eternity.

Chapter Sixteen

Ten days later Sara drove back from Carmel with a whirlwind of emotions bouncing back and forth inside her mind like a pinball machine. She had moments where she had been totally relaxed and distracted on the beach, reading and napping. And other times where she couldn't get her mind off Ian. She felt good with her decision of not going to Tiffany's wedding. It was time for her to grow up and end the competition with her. Ian had helped her see the light and she was grateful.

Then Becky had called Sara and had told her to come home immediately because she and Billy were going to get married. On the same day as Tiffany's wedding! After all that obsessing, Sara wouldn't have been able to go to Tiffany's wedding anyway, because there was no way she would miss Becky's wedding.

Then Becky asked Sara to be her maid of honor!

This was all happening so quickly.

Becky had explained that since it was going to be her second marriage she didn't want anything fancy or big—especially since all of her family and relatives lived in South Africa and wouldn't be able to make it. It would be a short ceremony at Cesar Chavez Park in downtown San Jose followed by a catered dinner across the street at the San Jose Tech Museum.

The emotions continued.

Sara was a little jealous that Becky was getting married.

I want to get married.

And just like that, her thoughts were back on Ian.

Kind Ian. Funny Ian. Sexy Ian.

She missed him so much and she wasn't going to be happy unless she was with him. She had to wake up before life and love passed her by. She moved next door to Ian for a reason, obviously.

To meet him.

No more fighting it. No more being a wimp. No more of that pathetic no-dating-neighbors crap she was obsessed with.

No more fear.

She was going to put her heart out there and she didn't care if someone stole it or stomped on it. The first thing she was going to do when she got home was march next door and bang on Ian's door. Then she would grab him, kiss the hell out of him, and tell him that she loved him. Or she could mention the love thing first and then kiss him after. The order didn't really matter. She also had to apologize for her insane accusations and for breaking the lighthouse.

She wiped her hands on her jeans—the thought of Ian made her hands sweat and she needed to be careful driving.

It kind of defeated the purpose of a plan to tell someone you loved him if you were going to die in a car crash before it happened.

She wiped her hands again on her jeans.

Where is all of this sweat coming from?

A little over an hour later she pulled up to her home, parked the car, and turned off the engine.

"Home, sweet home, Kili. You want to say hi to Ian?"

Kili leaned forward from the back seat and licked Sara on the shoulder.

"Of course you do."

Sara smiled and pulled the key halfway from the ignition and stopped. All of the energy drained from her body. She couldn't believe what she was looking at.

"No!"

She had no doubts a new emotion would surface any moment—an even stronger emotion—as she stared at the For Sale sign in front of Ian's house.

"Oh God, no," she said, continuing to stare at the sign. "He wants nothing to do with me. And I don't blame him."

It had been obviously a bad move to go away for so long without saying anything to Ian. She didn't tell him goodbye—didn't tell him the reason for going. Nothing. She just left. That must have been like a slap across the head to him. He took that as an obvious hint that she wanted nothing to do with him.

Ian pulled a play out of Sara's playbook. He couldn't live

next to Sara so he was moving away. He probably despised her.

Am I really that horrible that someone would move because of me?

Sara took Kili out of the car and to the birch tree for a pee. After Kili finished she pulled toward Ian's house and Sara wasn't going to deny the dog. Sara rang the doorbell and waited.

What was she going to say? She had no clue but she couldn't let him go. But what do you say to someone who doesn't want to see you, doesn't want to be with you? How do you convince them to stay? Especially when he must know she had been avoiding his phone calls.

Another mistake.

Ian didn't answer the door. Not a surprise.

She peeked through the window.

Oh my God.

All of his furniture was gone. He was gone. He already moved out. Even Kili's favorite planter box at the front door was gone. Nothing but a water ring where the base used to be.

Tears welled up in her eyes. This was her fault. She entered her home, trying to process what had happened. Her mind was too scattered and she couldn't focus on one thought. She tossed her dirty things in the clothes hamper and then she called Becky.

"She's back!" Becky answered, sounding as cheery as ever. Of course she would sound like that. The woman was getting married! "Did you go to Nordstrom yet?"

Becky had bought Sara what she called *the most beautiful maid of honor dress ever!* at Nordstrom and she needed to go pick it up.

Sara paced back and forth and sighed. "No. Not Yet. Soon." She sniffed.

"Have you been crying?"

"No!" She sniffed again. "Yes! Ian is gone and *I'm* an idiot."

"Gone? What are you talking about? He can't be gone because he's going to be at the wedding."

Sara stopped pacing and wiped her nose. "He is?"

"Of course."

She did loops around the kitchen table. "But he's selling his house."

"I don't know anything about that, but I do know he's going to be at the wedding since he's the best man."

"Seriously?"

"Of course! He's Billy's best friend!"

"Isn't that going to be awkward? You sure you want me to stand up for you?"

"Of course! Everything will be fine. You two are grown adults, I think you can handle it."

She didn't feel like a grown adult. She felt like a big baby. She needed to tell Ian how she felt but how was that going to go over when the man was trying to get away from her? "I'm going to throw up."

Becky laughed, forcing Sara to pull the phone away from her ear until the cackling ended.

"I'm not joking," said Sara.

"Relax. Everything will work out."

"How can I relax? Maybe I need some ice cream. Yeah, lots of ice cream."

"Don't you dare! You need to fit in that dress. Look, I've gotta run. Someone is trying to hem my dress while I wear it and I don't want to be stabbed to death. See you tomorrow!"

"Wait!" said Sara. She had a sudden case of guilt.

"What?" answered Becky.

"I'm sorry, I'm not being a good maid of honor. I should be supporting you and helping you but I'm being a baby."

"Hey, don't worry about it. I know you have a lot on your mind. The main thing is I want you to be next to me when I get married. You know I don't have a lot of friends and you're like family to me now. I met Billy, thanks to you and Ian. Like I said before everything will work out. Believe me."

"Thank you. I love you."

"I love you too. See you tomorrow."

Sara disconnected and smiled. For a brief moment her mind was off Ian. Becky was a wonderful friend with the big heart. Sara was happy for her. Happy that she could figure out so quickly that Billy was the right person for her.

Sara was convinced that Ian was the man for her too. Now if only she could convince *him* of that. Hopefully it wasn't too late.

*****

Billy stepped out of the dressing room at Macy's and did a spin for Ian. He adjusted the lapel and checked himself out in the mirror. "I think this is the one."

Ian eyed his dark blue suit and nodded. "You look great."

The salesman smiled. "It doesn't look like you'll need any alterations."

"Even better," said Billy. "I'll take it."

Ian pointed to his suit. "You know we're going to be wearing the exact same suits, right?"

Billy laughed. "No big deal. We'll have different color ties."

"Shall I bring you a few to choose from?" asked the salesman.

"That would be great, thank you."

The salesman walked away and Ian smiled at Billy. "Look at you, getting married. Just like that."

Billy grinned. "When you know, you know. Why delay it?"

"My grandfather said he knew he was going to marry my grandmother the day he met her. Actually, he said he knew after five minutes. That's crazy."

"I had the same feeling."

Ian's thoughts turned to Sara. That day they met he knew there was something special about her. She was beautiful inside and out. Sure, she had been a little crabby but she had a good reason to be since he had woken her up. And even though they had argued that morning he felt a spark. Immediately.

The last ten days without talking to Sara—without seeing her—had been pure torture. But she went away for a reason, to put space between them, and he had to respect that.

Billy frowned. "You okay?"

"Yeah. Sorry, man."

"Hey, no need to be sorry—you've got a lot going on. Thinking about Sara?"

Ian nodded. "I'm nervous about seeing her." He chuckled. "Not sure what I'm going to say."

The salesman returned and handed Billy a few ties.

"Thank you." Billy wrapped one of the ties around his neck and handed the others to Ian. "Just be yourself and tell her how you feel. That's all you can do."

"Yeah. Do you think I made the right decision?"

"I don't think you had any other choice."

Chapter Seventeen

Twenty-four hours later Billy and Ian stood near the fountain in Cesar Chavez Park in downtown San Jose with the wedding officiant, waiting for Becky and Sara to arrive. A small gathering of about thirty people were also standing nearby. It would be a simple ceremony. No music at all. Just the sound of the fountain, the cars driving by, the kids playing, and the planes flying overhead every three minutes since they were in the direct path of San Jose International Airport. There were no chairs for the guests to sit and no bridal party.

Ian knew he would want something a little more romantic and peaceful when he got married but he was happy for Billy and Becky. They were doing it exactly the way they wanted to do it.

    Any moment now a white Rolls Royce would pull up and double park by the curb to let the girls out. Then Sara and Becky would walk across the sidewalk, past the men playing backgammon, and down the path toward Billy and Ian. Ian was certain it would be in that very moment—the moment that he laid his eyes on Sara—that he would pass out and hit the cement. Hopefully he would come to in time for the ring exchange during the ceremony since he had both rings in his pocket.

Ian chewed on one of his fingernails and rocked back and forth, his weight shifting from one leg to the other. It wasn't cold so it didn't make sense why he was shaking.

Billy laughed and squeezed Ian's shoulder. "If you're imitating a Chihuahua, you've nailed it."

Ian pulled the finger from his mouth and wiped it on his pant leg. "Sorry."

"I'm the one getting married, remember?"

"Yeah. Sorry. I *am* happy for you. Let me try to focus on that."

The Rolls Royce pulled up and Sara stepped out, followed by Becky. They slowly made their way toward the fountain.

"She's beautiful," said Billy.

"Very," said Ian, who hadn't taken his eyes off Sara since she got out of the car. He felt guilty and glanced at Becky since she was the bride.

She looks nice. Okay, enough of that.

His eyes shot back to Sara. Beautiful Sara, wearing a turquoise dress with spaghetti straps. She also wore the silver necklace with the turquoise stone she bought at the art & wine festival. It was absolutely impossible for there to be a more beautiful woman than Sara.

Too bad she completely avoided eye contact with Ian.

Damn. She's still mad.

Becky and Sara arrived front and center and joined them.

A kid screamed and kicked water from the fountain but Billy and Becky weren't fazed by it. Ian wouldn't have even noticed either if it weren't for the water hitting his hand. He couldn't take his eyes off Sara. He wanted so much for her to look at him again. To give him a smile. Then and only then he would be able to relax a little. Billy took Becky's hand and smiled. That's when—finally!—Sara glanced at Ian and held his gaze.

Ian's heart rate kicked into overdrive; he couldn't look away. And when she gave him a tiny smile he sighed and relaxed his shoulders. He loved her smile.

Or was that smile for Billy and Becky? Damn, the sun was in his eyes.

His shoulders tensed again.

"Friends, it's great to have you here today," said the officiant. "I was told to warn you all ahead of time that this will be the shortest wedding ceremony ever, so don't blink."

The guests laughed and the officiant continued.

"Billy, do you want to marry Becky?"

"I do."

"And Becky, do you want to marry Billy?"

"I do."

"The rings please."

Wow. They weren't kidding when they said they wanted something simple. Glad I was paying attention.

Ian pulled the rings from the inside of his jacket pocket and handed them to the officiant.

Three minutes later Billy and Becky were married.

Ian couldn't believe it. Some people wait their whole lives and never meet the right person. Billy said something silly to a stranger at an art exhibition and married her a few weeks later.

Life was crazy.

Ian hugged his best friend and kissed Becky on the cheek. "Congratulations! I'm so happy for you both."

"Thanks, man," said Billy. "You're next!"

Sara was hugging Becky and froze. She looked back at Billy, then Ian.

Awkward.

Ian decided to not even comment.

The guests gathered around as more hugs, kisses, and congratulations were exchanged. The photographer had Becky and Billy pose for a few shots and then asked Sara and Ian to join them for a few more. Ian moved to Sara's side but the photographer directed him to stand on the other side next to Billy.

Damn.

A few more shots and they were done.

"Attention, everyone," yelled the photographer. "I'm going to steal the bride and groom away for a little bit for some pictures over at the Circle of Palms, so please head across the street to the Tech Museum to start the celebration.

Billy and Becky will be there shortly."

The guests did as they were told and walked in the direction of the museum.

Ian walked alongside Sara, but neither of them said a word. They waited at the crosswalk for the light to change so they could cross Market Street.

He glanced over at Sara. He could see eye movement, like she knew he was looking at her but she kept her focus on the stoplight.

He couldn't take the silence between them any longer and tried to break the ice with the first thing that came to his mind. "You're mean."

No! Why did you say that? Idiot!

Sara whipped her head around, hands on her hips. "Excuse me?"

God. If it were possible he would kick himself in the balls.

Where the hell did that come from? Idiot! Idiot! Idiot!

He wondered how he would recover from this blunder. He got nervous and repeatedly pressed the pedestrian button to cross. The only thing that would help him now was the green light and the sign that said *walk*.

Change. Change, please.

The light turned green.

"Yes!" he yelled, making Sara jump. They crossed the street and walked toward the entrance of the museum.

Sara sighed. "Please finish your thought."

The only option Ian had was to play dumb. "I don't know what you're talking about."

She shook her head. "Wimp."

He couldn't argue with her there.

They entered the museum and followed the signs to the reception area. There was a table near the entrance with an engagement picture of Billy and Becky on a beach with the Golden Gate Bridge in the background. On the same table were place cards for the meal.

Ian scanned the table for the card with his name on it and grabbed it. Table 2. Sara grabbed her card, also Table 2. Not a surprise since they were the best man and maid of honor. It made perfect sense that they would be sitting together at the same table.

Sara scratched the side of her face, studying the rest of the place cards. Then she turned around and stared at the tables. Ian followed her gaze and studied the room, trying to figure out what she was looking for.

A waiter arrived and offered them both a glass of wine from his tray. He took a sip of the wine, still trying to figure out what was going through Sara's mind. The woman was acting weird and he had no idea why.

"Is there a problem?" asked Ian.

"You'll see soon enough." She held up her glass to his. "Cheers."

*****

An hour later the DJ announced for everyone to take their seats. Sara had a chance to catch up with some former colleagues and enjoy some appetizers—bruschetta and coconut shrimp. But she now had a sudden rush of anxiety. She had been avoiding Ian during the cocktail hour but that was no longer possible since they were seated together.

She grabbed another glass of wine from the bar, took a giant gulp, and made her way to her table. *Their* table.

Ian was seated and looked nervous. When he saw Sara approach he sat up and brushed nonexistent crumbs from the table, then smacked the dinner roll from his plate to the floor. He jumped up and grabbed the roll from the floor and tossed it in the air a few times like he meant to do that. He placed the roll on the table, pulled Sara's chair out for her, and pointed to the seat. "Sit."

Sara stared at him. "I'm not a dog."

"Sorry. I don't know why I'm so nervous. Please have a seat."

Sara sat and was sure she was fidgeting as much as Ian now. It shouldn't be a surprise considering the bride and groom stuck them at a table for two!

She couldn't believe this. Becky and Billy had this planned. Obviously Ian wasn't involved in this seating scheme since he was in the process of selling his house to get away from her. Plus, he looked as uncomfortable as she did.

Sweetheart tables were common at weddings for the

bride and groom. But for the best man and the maid of honor? Never!

"Friends and family," said the DJ. "Please welcome the bride and groom, Mr. and Mrs. Hill!"

Sara leaned in to Ian. "Billy Hill?"

Ian nodded. "In school the kids used to call him hillbilly."

Sara snort-laughed and checked her nose to make sure wine hadn't shot out.

Good. All clear.

The guests clapped and cheered. Becky and Billy entered and waved to everyone, making their way toward their seats. They looked so happy.

Billy looked in the direction of Ian and Sara and winked.

Was he winking at me or Ian or both of us?

Ian raised his glass toward Becky and Billy and bowed his head slightly. Then he took a sip of his wine and started shifting back and forth in his seat.

"You fidget a lot," Sara.

"You're one to talk, Miss Fidgety McFidget," said Ian.

"Ha! I'm as relaxed as ever," she lied, taking another gulp of her wine.

"Uh huh."

"And you need to explain yourself."

Ian turned to her. "What do I need to explain?"

Men.

"You called me mean," Sara said. She tried giving him

her best pouty face but she had a feeling she looked more deformed, if anything.

"Ahhh. That." He took a sip of his wine. "That was a temporary stoppage of intelligence and I take it back."

"You can't take it back."

Ian set down his glass of wine. "If I buy a television and don't like it, can I take it back?"

"Of course."

"So…I didn't like what I said to you and take it back."

"That's ridiculous."

"That shouldn't be a surprise since you know I specialize in ridiculousness."

Sara laughed and threw her hand over her mouth. "Don't make me laugh. I'm mad at you."

"Why?"

Maybe if she stared at him long enough he would figure it out. Nope. Nothing. She didn't like being called mean. Better to keep asking him why he called her that until he caved in. That seemed like the mature thing to do.

"You think I'm mean," she said. "Tell me why."

He sat up. "Fine. I'll tell you. Because you just disappeared."

"Yeah?"

"Yeah."

"You did the same thing!"

"When?"

"Have you seen your house lately? The one with the For

Sale sign in front? The place is empty and *you* disappeared."

"I—"

"The buffet is now open," said the DJ. "Please help yourselves."

Sara and Ian dropped the subject and headed to the buffet for food. They each grabbed a plate and arrived at the salads, inspecting them.

"By the way, you look beautiful," said Ian out of left field.

Sara blushed. "Thank you, but please do not compliment me."

"Why not?"

"Because it confuses me."

"Fine. You look like a monkey."

"Oh!" Sara grabbed a helping of beet salad and plopped it on Ian's plate.

"What are you doing? I don't like beets."

"Eat them. They're good for your colon. Especially helpful since you have your head up your—"

"Wow!" said Becky, cutting in front of Sara with her plate. "The food looks lovely!" She placed a spoonful of rice pilaf on her plate and winked at Sara. "How are you two doing?"

"I'm just peachy," said Sara. "I'm *especially* enjoying the interesting seating arrangements you have this evening."

"Yeah," said Ian. "Who was the genius who thought of that?"

Becky and Billy looked at each other and both shrugged.

"Of course," said Ian. "It happened all by itself."

Billy grabbed a piece of Chicken Marsala, then said loudly to Becky, "It looks like *some*body needs to get laid."

Becky also grabbed a piece of the chicken and glanced at Sara. "I'd say it's more than one person. You kids have fun!"

Sara didn't need to get laid. Okay, that was a lie. The truth was she would love to wake up next to that sexy man beside her in line. Her initial plan was to come back from Carmel and grab him and kiss him. Then tell him she loved him. But Ian putting his house up for sale and moving away kind of changed things. His actions had spoken. The strange part was, he wasn't talking about it or at least trying to explain himself.

Ian and Sara had barely spoken a word during the dinner. Just a couple of musings about the food and how the Tech Museum was the perfect place for their two nerdy friends to celebrate. And Ian also asked how Kili was. That was it.

"Excuse me," said Ian to Sara, getting up and walking over to the DJ. She watched as they chatted for a moment.

What is he doing?

The DJ nodded and handed Ian a microphone.

"Hello?" said Ian, talking into the microphone. "Okay, good." He cleared his throat. "I'm Ian McBride and I'm Billy's best man. Since it's customary, I wanted to toast the newlyweds." He paced a little, looking like he was trying to gather his thoughts. "I used to think relationships were naturally difficult but now I've realized that they aren't difficult at all. Loving someone is easy. We are the ones who make things difficult."

"You got that right," said Sara, a little too loudly.

The guests laughed and Sara's hand flew up to cover her mouth. Her face must have been as bright as that beet salad she had earlier. She couldn't believe she said that out loud.

"Glad you agree," said Ian, chuckling. "Anyway, I wanted to say that I've learned a lot by watching Becky and Billy these last few weeks. We can all see how happy they are. They're made for each other. They didn't listen to what friends or family or society said about jumping into things and I admire that in them. A wise person once told me sometimes you just have to go for what you want."

Wait, I said that. He's calling me wise? And he called me beautiful at the buffet. What is wrong with this man?

"Becky and Billy have done that," continued Ian. "They went for it and look at them, so happy." Ian raised his glass of wine. "To love, laughter, and going for what you want. Cheers."

The guests yelled "cheers" in unison. Ian set his wine on the table and hugged and kissed Billy and Becky.

Ian sat back down next to Sara and smiled.

She returned his smile and held out her glass. "That was a wonderful toast. Cheers."

"Thanks. Cheers." They toasted and he took a sip of his

wine.

Sara crossed her arms. "And who was this wise person you spoke of?"

"The most amazing woman."

He needed to quit sending her mixed signals. It was going to drive her crazy and she was getting that urge to grab him and kiss him again.

"And on that note," said the DJ. "Please welcome Billy and Becky to the dance floor for their first dance!"

The DJ played "All of Me" from John Legend. Billy and Becky danced and it reminded Sara of the dance she shared with Ian at the art & wine festival.

Holy cow, what a dance that was.

Half way through the song the DJ made another announcement. "Becky and Billy would like the rest of you to join them at this time to finish out the dance."

Ian looked in Sara's direction and her heart nearly exploded.

He extended his hand to hers. "Looks like that's our cue."

Sara stared at his hand but couldn't get any words out.

"Come on," said Ian. "Take my hand."

"Not gonna do it."

"Take it."

She crossed her arms. "No."

"Chicken."

"Ha!" said Sara. A couple of heads turned in her

direction and she lowered her voice. "You're the one who's a big chicken—you couldn't handle the heat. But instead of getting out of the kitchen you *sold* it, along with the entire house. It's obvious you don't want anything to do with me."

"I'm willing to pretend."

Her double take was so forceful she almost dislodged her head. "Huh?"

"I'll pretend I want to dance with you and *you'll* pretend you want to dance with me. They asked us to join them, so we are doing this for them. Do you really want to let them down?"

His hand was still extended and she stared at it.

She huffed like Kili would. "Fine."

"Better than fine," he answered.

"Good."

"Great."

"Fine."

He smirked. "You already said that."

Sara took Ian's hand and he led her to the dance floor. She was playing hard to get but who was she kidding? She couldn't resist being in his arms.

Ian placed his hand on the small of her back and pulled her close.

Oh God, this feels so good. It feels like home.

Sara relaxed into his chest. They swayed back and forth and she listened to John Legend sing about love and people with imperfections. She had her share of imperfections, everyone did. But right now none of that mattered. She loved where she was, in Ian's arms. It was heaven on earth.

He pulled her even closer—they were now cheek to cheek. "You smell nice."

"Thanks," she said.

Ian looked into her eyes. "I'm sorry for yelling at you and Kili that morning. And I'm going to apologize to her too. I'll bring a toy or her favorite plant to eat."

Sara laughed.

"Please forgive me," said Ian.

"Only if you forgive me for not trusting you and for breaking the lighthouse."

"Done."

She sighed. "Good."

He pulled her close, cheek to cheek again, and whispered in her ear. "I love you."

Huh? Did he say what I think he said?

Sara didn't think it was possible for her heart to beat any faster. She didn't respond. How could he say that to her now? That wasn't fair. He was moving!

She had to know. "If you love me why are you moving?"

"It was the most logical thing for me to do."

Not logical to me at all. "Please explain," she said.

"It's simple. You said you don't date your neighbors. I'm not your neighbor anymore. We can date now."

Sara swallowed hard. "Oh…"

"No more excuses. No more pretending. What we have is

real, you and me. Me and you." A tear fell down her face and he caught it with his thumb. "So I'm going to tell you again right now. And then I will tell you again a million more times in the future. I love you."

Another tear. "I love you too and I can't take it anymore. Please kiss me."

Ian grinned and lowered his head, pressing his lips to hers. It's what she wanted. What she needed.

Ian pulled away from the kiss. "I want to return to your kiss because it's the sweetest thing I've ever tasted, but I had to mention what you did was amazing. Going to Cambria, buying that other lighthouse, that was kind beyond words. Thank you."

"You're welcome. And by the way, you're not going to believe this."

Ian kissed Sara on her forehead. "Try me."

"While I was away I had made up my mind to date neighbors. To date you."

"You're right, I don't believe it."

"Oh!" Sara pinched Ian in his side and he laughed. "I'm telling you the truth!"

"Look, I get the credit for us being together. End of story."

"If that's what makes you and your male ego happy, fine."

"Glad we settled that. You see that? Our arguments are getting shorter. That's a good sign."

The DJ played another slow song. "A Thousand Years" from Christina Perri.

"I love this song. Let's keep dancing!"

"I don't have a problem with that." Ian grinned and spun her around, but then suddenly dropped her hand.

"What?" asked Sara.

"I've been waiting for the right moment for this and now would be perfect." He reached into his jacket pocket.

What does he have in his pocket? Something for me?

"Close your eyes and stick out your hand."

Sara blinked and then looked around the room. "Now?"

"Of course now. Do it."

She closed her eyes and he grabbed her hand.

It can't be a ring. That would be crazy.

She felt him wrap something around her wrist.

A bracelet? I love bracelets!

"Okay, open your eyes," he said.

Sara opened her eyes and stared at her wrist. "Oh my God." It was the beautiful bracelet that she tried on at the art & wine festival. She blinked a couple of times. "But I don't get it. How did you…?"

Ian shrugged.

She adjusted the bracelet and smiled. "I can't believe you did that. This is so precious, thank you." She reached up and kissed him on the lips. "And by the way, you don't have to sell your house."

"Too late."

She did a double take. "Really?"

Ian filled Sara in on the latest about his home, that an offer had come in and he had accepted it. And that he was going into business with Krasimir. His dream of having a gallery was going to come true.

"And it's all because of you," he said. "We found the perfect property in downtown Campbell for the gallery and it has a large living space upstairs. I can't wait to show you."

Sara felt another set of arms around her. Then another.

Becky and Billy were wrapped around Sara and Ian.

Billy smiled. "How are you kids doing? Good?"

"You both think you're so smart, don't you?" said Ian.

Becky nodded. "*I* certainly do."

"Hey, *I'm* a genius," said Billy. "I do remember you calling me that earlier."

Ian shook his head. "I take it back."

Becky and Billy laughed and broke away from Ian and Sara, finishing their dance alone.

"There you go, trying to take things back again," said Sara. "Say something and don't take it back."

"I love you."

Sara smiled. "I like the way that sounds. Say it again."

"I love you." Ian kissed her. "You approve?"

"Much better," Sara answered.

"Good."

"Great."

"Perfect.

"Better than perfect."

"Good."

Sara poked Ian in the chest. "You already said that!"

<<<<<>>>>>

A Note From Rich

Dear Reader,

Thanks so much for taking the time to read my third novel, *Kissing Frogs*. I hope you enjoyed Sara and Ian's story. It was a lot of fun to write and I'm still amazed that I get to do this for a living.

I would be so grateful if you would take the time to leave a review online at Amazon and Goodreads. It would mean the world to me and would also help new readers find my stories.

Visit my website at http://www.richamooi.com to learn about my other romantic comedies.

And feel free to send me an email to say hello! I love to hear from my readers—it motivates me and helps me write faster. :) My email address is rich@richamooi.com.

All the best,

Rich

Acknowledgements

It takes more than a few people to publish a book so I want to send out a big THANK YOU to everyone who helped make *Kissing Frogs* possible.

To my scorching hot wife, Silvi, who read this story three times at various stages. YOU ROCK, BABY!

To Mary Yakovets for editing. Thanks so much for your hard work—especially for getting rid of the five thousand commas that were slowing the story down.

To Robert Roffey, Isabel Anievas, Krasimir Sofijski, Laura de la Prida, and Julita Sofijski. Thank you for your friendship, your support, and your help.

To fellow authors Deb Julienne, Hannah Jayne, Claire Frank, CeeCee James, Myra Scott, Simone Pond, Tammi Labrecque, and Christine Mancuso for your help.